Speaking Of Romance

A COLLECTION OF SHORT STORIES

Table
of Contents

Publisher Page... *ii*

1 **Finally Becoming His Lady -** Carnation.......................................1

2 **High School Drama -** Meghan Giannotta 12

3 **Hiraeth -** Danielle Chan..25

4 **I Never Wear White -** Mel Buckingham..31

5 **Island Boy -** Leonie Milde...35

6 **Lover's Reunion -** Micah Brocker..49

7 **The Orange Grove -** Rose McCoy...53

8 **Walter Goes On A Date -** C. W. Toledo...64

9 **Who Will Be My Love? -** K. A. Baker 110

10 **Love Of My Life -** Roy Kindelberger..117

11 **One Night -** Kieran McLoughlin 119

Acknowledgements... *124*

Participants In Contest & Winners *125*

Gift A Copy Of This Book To A Friend... *127*

Send Us A Book Review *128*

Finally Becoming His Lady

Carnation

Garland, Texas - United States

By nighttime, Thomas Winn, a university student, had finished most of his homework as well as his dinner, in which both had been put away. He was inside his bedroom; the door was closed and locked in place and the bed had neatly tucked sheets, where the blanket was folded on top of it with the pillow aligned in its usual spot. He sat own on his chair facing his computer desk. The clock had reached after nine o'clock, but still—he opened a browser on Facebook, and slowly slid the mouse to his chat box.

He typed some words.

Thomas Winn: […Hey. Can you meet up with me tomorrow? I need help with something that's bothering me.]

There was a young woman named Brenda Carmine online, whom many people (besides Thomas) would go to for their love and relationship problems. As her surname suggested, she had a deep red hue to her hair, yet her eyes were light green. She seemed like a fair lady too as she replied.

Brenda Carmine: [Alright. I'll be available around 10 A.M. Does that sound good to you? We can have our chat in the café that's located upstairs in your school's dining hall.]

Thomas Winn: [You do understand that it's not an actual café, but just a food court with lots of tables, don't you? It's just like being in a smaller version of a mall. Nothing special about it. Just an ordinary place for ordinary people.]

Brenda Carmine: [Really, you don't have to put it that way. I, for instance, actually like the vibe younger people such as yourself, give off whenever I'm visiting. It's quite soothing for my soul.]

Thomas sighed after he read that message. It had seemed as though Brenda's "voice" was amused with his lack of humor. He went back to typing.

Thomas Winn: [What's so funny to you? I'm the one who has to deal with my problem, but it's difficult. You should know better than to pick with me.]

"Oh, dear me~!" Brenda giggled in her office. She was sitting at a burnt umber desk, with her rear end planted on a matching rolling chair.

Inside, it was dark and the only light source was the gold platinum Samsung Galaxy S6 in her hands. Although there were bookshelves of a burgundy color against the walls, nothing else furnished the room.

"Perhaps, I shouldn't mess with him so much," she mused. "Not that I can help myself. Thomas is too serious for his own good."

Shortly afterward, a response from Brenda entered the chat box.

Brenda Carmine: [Never mind my teasing, Thomas. I've already settled a time and place for our appointment. I'm a very busy woman, so an opportunity such as this may not knock on your door for another few weeks—even months—at that.]

While it showed that Thomas was typing, Brenda could sense a tad bit of irritation from him. However, it did not displease her, but made her laugh lightly.

"Ahaha, how tense must he be with me?" she asked. "This poor lad must be more confused than the barber from next door."

Thomas finally stopped typing and entered his message.

Thomas Winn: [Woman, please. I barely had a chance to do the arrangement for our meeting. In fact, I didn't have a say in finding my own time for an appointment. I don't believe a client shouldn't have a say in what time is available in their schedule. This makes the situation like a fraudulent business transaction—a scam. What are you trying to pull this time, Brenda?]

Brenda Carmine: [Ahaha, nothing, dear! Why don't you get some rest at the moment? I'll see you when you're ready to complain to me about your issue, or issues. Toodles!]

It took a few seconds for the redhead to go offline. Thomas sighed again and slumped backward in his chair.

"What's the point of avoiding my question?" he said to himself. "She couldn't possibly be *that* busy if she had time to go on social media." He closed his eyes to allow another short pause to take place. "I don't understand women very well, I suppose. I mean, how would I?—Especially with—"

His silver rectangular flip phone vibrated, indicating that someone had texted him. The next thing he knew, he opened his eyes, grabbed the mobile device in a gentle manner, and checked his messages.

"Speak of the devil herself," he muttered.

The text he had checked was from a girl called Felicity Valentine, and the thought of her had stirred in Thomas' soul like a flame that continued to fuel up and expand. In a sense, it was as if that flame dangerously spread out and encompassed a forest on its path to destruction; albeit, Thomas didn't mean to consider receiving a text from his female companion as a bad thing. Still, it read:

[I've heard some rumors lately… Is it true that you have a girl that you like?]

"What great timing for her to ask about herself," he muttered under his breath. Nearly all of his will to stay awake that night had drained in an instant. It wasn't the fact it was a message from Felicity, he attempted to reason with himself. It was the worn-out frustration of dealing with her words.

Doesn't she remember the last the we talk about something like this? He asked in his mind. His shoulders fell while he sighed profoundly. *No, I suppose she wouldn't. Not with the way she is…*

However, he sent his answer: "I'll let you know another time." Thomas trudged to his bed and plopped dreadfully onto it. Afterwards, he took out a small remote control from under his blanket that controlled the lights, and pressed a button near the bottom to switch the lights off. It took several seconds before he fell asleep in his haggard state.

~ ~ ~

The following morning, Thomas met up with Brenda in his university's cafeteria. It was like any other day; he didn't put any effort in dressing up, so he had worn his brown stuffed up coat over a white V-neck shirt, which made him resemble a medium-bellied turkey—alive but he usually didn't look cheery. It was a hilarious sight to see, even with his black slacks and tan loafers over his eggshell white socks.

Sitting at a table near the stairwell, Brenda was waving jovially with her right arm and hand. "Woohoo! Thomas~! You're looking more like a fine piece of poultry these days, aren't you?" Intriguingly, she had a jade beaded bracelet around her wrist, a violet long-sleeve blouse over a pair of red pants, and cloud gray flats covering her feet.

"Oh, can it, will you?" Thomas grunted. "My jacket's got nothing to do with my actual physique. And what's with the way you're dressed? Are you some crystal ball fortune-teller?"

"Ah, yes," Brenda nodded with her eyes closed. "Anyone who's seen you without it knows your abdomen is flat like a slab of meat angrily slapped onto a slice of bread while someone's in the process of preparing a sandwich." She shrugged and opened her eyes with a frown. "It's a shame you don't allow many people to see you without your pitiful jacket. When we first met, you seemed brighter—obviously, you didn't have it back then, but… Anyhow, lighten up a little and tell me your problem."

"Alright," Thomas said quietly. He slowly strolled to where the small table was and took the empty seat across from Brenda.

"Let's start our session, shall we?" Brenda beamed. "You've got fifteen minutes. Well, no, I'll be generous enough to extend it by another ten. So, twenty-five minutes. Begin, young lad."

Thomas sighed and began his rant as instructed. "I told the girl I like about my feelings once; she didn't say yes or no to me—even told me that she appreciates the sentiment and all, but I knew at that moment that she was holding back."

The image of a pure, yet downcast-eyed girl with brunette hair that extended down to her waist appeared in his mind. She had a full set of bangs that covered her left eye, but were diagonally cut to show her right one. Because it was cold outside (and it was Valentine's Day of the previous year), she had worn a thick black scarf with bronze, diamond-shaped rhinestones, a dark green hoodie with long sleeve covering up to a large portion of the palm of her hands, royal purple leggings, and a pair of fuzzy black ankle boots. Felicity was so petite in stature that a tall guy like Thomas had to lean down a little to look at her, but he couldn't see much of her hazel right eye. However, they were both the same age and in the same year at their university.

As her fingers fidgeted, her small voice articulated. "U-Um, I-I'm r-r-really s-sorry Thomas. I, um.. c-can't return your f-feelings for me, b-but I a-actually a-a-appreciate them. I r-really do, but…"

Unfortunately, Felicity turned around and her tiny feet took off. She wasn't sprinting, but she was running as fast as she could. Thomas could not make out a sound, but he watched with a tinge of regret at denting their friendship. Just because he confessed how he felt to the girl he wanted to be with, it didn't mean she would accept him.

Returning to the reality of having his heart resonating with a dull dose of pain, he thought, *That's right, isn't it? She didn't accept the heart I exposed to her. She would never have in the first place. Not once did she ever… look at me with the eyes of romance, but with those of a good friend. Good, but never close to each other. Not even our friendship had ever been that tightly bundled together.*

Thomas sighed dejectedly, staring down at the table's glittering, smooth surface. "Her anxiety traps her into a state where she becomes depressed after overthinking and believing she can't do anything worthwhile. Yesterday, she messaged me wondering if there's someone I like. Not only is she oblivious, but she's become so forgetful of the fact I stated, 'I like you' to her before. The situation I've experienced is terrible, Brenda…"

Brenda smiled sympathetically at her client's self-pity. Somehow, she wanted to reach her hand out to pet him like anyone would for a puppy or an older dog. It was heart-warming for her to see him in such as sad state, but she told him, "In contrast to her anxiety, she could have developed a defense mechanism, young lad." Once Thomas looked up at her, the redhead added, "You ought to comprehend her better as a friend. She's been suffering for quite a while with her anxiety that she's become the poor victim. Anxiety may seem like the monster of the heart, but it's the servant of a true demon, and that is called the defense mechanism. They act as a barrier that someone unconsciously uses to protect themselves. I don't find them to be shields for people, rather they're more like cages that prevent salvation from imprisonment. Perhaps all you need to do for both of your sakes, is to tell her your feelings once again. You're more confident than she is, so become the person who'll support her, my darling client."

"I see," Thomas nodded after gazing into his confidante's eyes, which appeared to him as an earnest ray of hope telling him it wasn't over. He still had time to rekindle his friendship with Felicity and perhaps someday, he could find another chance to confess once more to her. "Thanks, Brenda."

"No need to thank me. I'm rooting for you to win your battle; no pun intended from your surname, of course." The woman left her seat and exited the university food court.

Once Brenda was out of sight, Thomas took out his cell phone from his pants pocket and stared at it for a few seconds. Then again, he had stalled and avoided replying to Felicity's text for a while now. He opened his device and types out the words:

[Yeah, I guess you could say that.]

He frowned at his formality with using "could" instead of "can" for his reply, but he knew it wasn't simple to heal the wound to his own heart.

Indeed, mustering up his courage at a time when he didn't want to be rejected all over again was the safer choice, one that would lead to a safer route, so to speak. He added on another line in the message.

[Never mind. Why don't we meet up as usual later? It'll be my treat.]

After he pressed "send" there was an instant message back.

[Oh. Well, okay. I can meet you any time after 4:30 P.M. Is that okay with you?]

Thomas blink. How would he stall for time from her? Since it was Felicity on the other end of their text conversation, it wasn't so easy to come up with more replies.

It took from a few seconds to a few minutes. But… he finally responded.

[Sure, but I can make it after 6:45 instead.]

He nodded to himself. *As a guy, I should also be there to groom myself and make sure I look nice.* He shook his head and facepalmed right over his eyes and forehead with his free hand. *What am I thinking?! I don't even have facial or body hair; I'm smooth all over! Gah! I gotta think about my dress code now.* Taking a deep breath, he calmed down a little. *Alright… Let's start over. Hmm. Casual, casual. Just what is casual anymore?*

As he gave another shake from his head, another message was sent to his phone.

[…I guess you'd rather be with the girl you like before hanging out with me. Sorry for being so bothersome, Thomas.]

Dense, he thought. *Too dense for her own good. Great… What do I do now?*

He sighed, but couldn't help but type out another reply.

[It's okay, Felicity. I'm not meeting anyone other than you. It's our day every time we see each other, you know?]

[But I don't want to be rude to the girl you like.]

[I'm sure someday she'll decide on what to do about her own feelings. Telling her once was already enough to make her get cold feet, so I'll wait for her to come around.]

[I see. I hope things go well. I'll see you later.]

After Felicity's final message to him, Thomas let out a groan.

"Arrrggghhhh."

He decided to sleep. Sleep like there was no tomorrow even though it would arrive. Then, he would decide how to dress. After all, the school itself was close to his home.

~ ~ ~

Several hours later, Thomas took Felicity to a coffee shop not too far from campus, but stopped in front of the door, leaving the girl perplexed. He was dressed in a black pull-over jacket, marron pants, and a pair of red sneakers. Felicity, on the other hand, was wearing a sweater that was green and gold with a reindeer on the front. She also had on gray jeans, a pair of brown knee-high boots, and a charcoal knit hat on her head.

"Huh?" Felicity blinked. To Thomas, she seemed somewhat different—changed than she was before. "Why're you standing here? Let's go in already!"

"Hold on," Thomas urged. "I need to say this to your dense face. Look, you already erased this from your memories, but I told you a while back that I like you, not as a friend, but as a man. I don't expect you to reciprocate my feelings, so I'd rather not end our friendship over some stupid confession I made that may have placed you in a discomforting situation with me. I don't like any other girl than you, you blockhead."

The brunette cast her eyes unto the ground and frowned. "Honestly, I was lying when I sent you that text. I know it's my fault you had to say it again, but I couldn't believe that I'd make a good girlfriend for you, Thomas. I kept telling myself that there'd be no way we could be together with how I am." Raising her head, she apologized. "Sorry for causing you trouble. If you're really willing to forgive me, I can become your actual lover now."

A genuine smile spread across Thomas's visage. "…You said it." He opened the door for his source of happiness—his lady.

High School Drama

Meghan Giannotta

Auburn, New York - United States

Hi my name is May, I am starting my first day of 10th grade today. I recently just moved here from Chicago. I am incredibly nervous because I am going into school knowing no one. My goal this year is to just keep my grades up and study really hard to make my parents proud. Of course I also want to make friends along the way. My Mom calls me downstairs for breakfast and my stomach is in knots. My long brown straight hair is not laying the way I need it to. I have to look my best for the first day and nothing is going my way. Today has to be perfect. I have to make a good first impression. Everyone already has their friends and their groups and I am starting from scratch.

"May come down here your breakfast is getting cold," my mother calls out.

I guess my hair looks fine, so I walk downstairs and sit at the table. My Mom made me scrambled eggs, toast and a cup of orange juice on the side. I told her everything looked great but I was just so nervous I could not eat. She told me to at least have some toast I could not go to school on an empty stomach. She sat down next to me and told me everything will be fine. I had tons of friends at my old school and everyone loved me. Mom had no doubt at all in her mind I would make friends today. Shortly after, I was on my way to school.

Walking into school my heart was pounding so fast. As soon as I walked in I could immediately see all the different groups everyone was in. Everyone already had their cliques and groups and I was in the middle of no man's land. I was terrified and I was only two steps in the doorway. I tried saying Hi! to people with a hope they would say Hi! but nothing exciting, no interest in wanting to be my friend. I knew this would be the longest day of my life, and I for one was not ready for it.

My mom always said you are never ready for anything, you just must dive right in and conquer the world. So that is exactly what I did, or I at least tried to.

My teacher started talking, handing out schedules. Everyone was comparing classes with each other but all I could do was see if I could figure out where my classes were. The bell rang and it finally set in. I had to go to my first class. I walked to class and sat in the second row. I figured that was the safest, not completely in the front so I look like a teacher's pet but not in the back where I could not see anything. I sit next to this girl, blonde, super tall, blue eyes, and seems to be wearing a cheerleader uniform. I wonder if there is a game tonight. Maybe I will go and see what it is all about.

Hey, my name is May. What is yours? "Margaret," the young girl says.

Then I heard from a distance "Margaret get over here, what do you think you are doing talking with the new girl"

I overheard this girl whispering to Margaret and I was so confused like what could I have possibly done wrong already. It was my first day. I heard Margaret whisper to apparently my new enemy

"Kiley, she just asked me my name. What did you want me to do to ignore her?" Margaret questioned Kiley.

Kiley eventually spoke out after thinking for a minute "No I guess not but if she thinks she is becoming friends with us she has another thing coming." I kept questioning if I should go up to this Kiley girl and ask her what I could have possibly done to get on her enemy list already. It is not even 10:00. By the time I had the slightest bit of courage to go up to her she had already left.

I wondered who this Kiley girl really even is. Does she have some title that just decides if the new kids gets an in or not? Who does she think she is? The real question is where can I go to find more information about this girl? I thought to myself and the only obvious choice that came to my mind was the library hoping they have previous yearbooks in there.

Once 12:00 hit I went to the library, of course I got lost along the way. This school is huge! Once I found it I sat down at a table and pulled out my lunch. I had a feeling I would be eating my lunch in here often considering I have no friends but maybe things will change. Once I was settled I went over to the librarian and politely asked if they had yearbooks from previous years anywhere. She pointed me in a certain direction and I found them!

The way this school works is people from grade 9 through grade 12 are in this building so I really had no clue what I was working with. The worst thing that could happen was she could be a freshman and there would be nothing on her. If she was a freshman she would have some nerve talking to me. I walk over to the bookcase and pull out some yearbooks. I scope out the yearbooks and stumble across the freshman page from last year meaning this is everyone in my grade. I flip through the pages scanning intensely to find Kiley.

All of a sudden I stumble across the cheer page and there she is. Her long blonde hair in the highest ponytail imaginable with a huge glowing blue bow. I looked through the names to find out Kiley was on the varsity cheerleading team as a freshman. Just as I thought things couldn't get any worse she was the cheer captain. I closed the book and just finished the rest of my lunch.

I go to my next class and see she is in it. The teacher starts writing multiplication questions on the board and asks if anyone knows the answers. Math is my specialty so I was getting all the questions right. I see Kiley staring into my soul. Then I heard her whisper something to her friends but I was too far away and could not hear anything they said. All I could hear was laughter. I thought to myself this is going to be a long year. I already have enemies and I have no clue what I even did! I just thought to myself maybe if I focus on school this year I will be okay, but then I thought to myself. I cannot go a whole year without any friends. I need to put myself out there.

The next day I walked into school with the cutest outfit I could find. My goal was to make at least one friend today. I walk downstairs and eat all of my breakfast then scurry off to school. My school is only a few blocks away so I just walk. On my walk to school I listen to pump up music to get me excited for a new day.

I walk into school feeling confident as ever I walk into the building to scope out who I was going to be friends with. I said my hellos and asked people what their names were but more and more people were shying away from me and I could not figure out why but all I could think was Kiley had something to do with it.

I decided to go to the cafeteria today and decided maybe if I sat at an empty seat at a lunch table people would talk to me. As soon as I walked in and looked for seats every single person said to me "This seat is taken, sorry." I am genuinely just so confused on how every seat is taken but whatever.

I make my way to the library. I find a table in the corner and pull out a book to read while I eat my sandwich. I hear a voice talking to the librarian. I look up and see this boy wearing a football jacket with the letter C on it. He is the most attractive boy I have ever seen in my entire life. This was my time. We were the only two in the library and I could finally make a friend. As soon as I am about to get up, my stomach turns into knots. This is the same feeling I felt when I started my first day of school here. Of course when I need to have the most confidence I have the least. I can only hope that I see him at the library again.

I finish the rest of my day minding my business avoiding Kiley and just focusing on my work trying to not get behind. The rest of the day I was just so frustrated no one wanted to be my friend and it was all Kiley's fault. This is so annoying. Why should I let her ruin my high school experience? I am so over high school already and I just started.

I walked home and my mom asked, "How was school sweetie?" Of course I did not want to tell her how miserable I was there. I do not want to make her sad. "School is fine Mom." Keeping it short and sweet. My only hope was the cute boy.

The next day it was the same routine. I got up and walked to school and had no expectations at this point for making friends. I went to my morning classes then once it hit 12 I went to the library and finished the rest of my day.

A few weeks later. . . .

The homecoming dance is coming up and I still have no friends. I need to figure something out. There is no way I am missing my first homecoming dance.

I went to the library to brainstorm a plan of how I am going to make friends. Sure enough I hear a voice that sounds very familiar. I looked up and there he was. I heard the librarian say "Thank you Brad" and I looked up and there he was. What should I do? Do I ask him if he is going to homecoming? Do I ask him to go to the dance with me? Do people even take dates to this kind of dance? Ugh he is coming over here I have to act cool.

"Hey" Brad said with a smile. Hi I am May. "I am Brad, nice to meet you."

For the rest of the day that was all I could think of. He was so dreamy his smile could light up a room.

I walked into math class and sure enough Kiley was there giving me an evil death glare like always. "Ugh why are you so smiley today? What did you finally make a friend?" Kiley said with her usual attitude

Well Kiley it is not really your business but yes I did make a friend today so I guess not everyone in the school listens to you after all. Is what I wanted to say but I just said no I just did well on my English exam that's all.

The next day I go to the library and Brad is there. "Hey May, mind if I sit with you?"

Oh of course not Brad! "I noticed you don't really have any friends yet, do you?" "No not really this girl is kinda like turning everyone away from me and I really do not know why she has been doing this since the first day I got here." "What the heck, why would she do that, who is that?" Brad questioned. I thought about it for a second and I was gonna tell Brad her name but I was just like whatever I am not getting her even more mad at me. I just said oh I am not really sure I think she is in my math class though. Then I just dropped the conversation. I didn't really want to get in more drama than I already am in.

The next day sure enough I go to the library and sure enough Brad is there already sitting at the table I usually sit at. That happened the rest of the week. I thought about asking him to the dance but I looked it up. Apparently people do not ask other people out on homecoming. So for right now I will settle with just being friends with him for now.

That weekend my mom and I spent the whole weekend finding the perfect dress, finding the perfect nail polish, everything must be perfect next weekend. Even though I still do not have friends, a few girls did invite me to go with them. I was so excited I could not wait for the dance next weekend. Even though I did not ask Brad to the dance, maybe we could get a picture together.

My mom and I went to store after store until we found the perfect dress. Once we found the perfect dress we moved onto the shoe store. We easily spent two hours at the store and then I saw the perfect pair. 3 inches maybe 4 all black with a sparking heel. Perfect I said. Now we have to make one of the most important decisions. Nail color. I decided to go with a red one. I felt like that was the safest choice.

I went to school that Monday and finally did not sit at the library, I found the girls who I was going to dance with and sat with them. The next thing I know I look over and see Brad sitting with Kiley at the lunch table. Maybe they are just friends, she is very popular after all.

I find my friends and I sit next to them. Everyone was talking about the dance and how excited they were that I was going with them! The whole lunch period we were talking about what color our dress was and what color nail polish we were getting. Then we talked about what time to get to Darcie's house.

Once the day ended I went straight home and told my mom how I finally ate in the cafeteria! "That is great sweety I am so glad you are starting to make friends" My mom said while she was getting comfortable on the couch. She looked like she was going to be there for the rest of the night

Later that night I debated about asking my new friends if they knew anything about Brad and Kiley but I figured I would just rather not know.

The next day I went to school and I had a test later in the day so I went to the library to study. Brad was also in the library and he sat at the table with me. "Hey May, I have a question," Brad said as he approached me.

Oh hey Brad whats up.

"You are going to the homecoming dance right?"

"Yeah of course I am. It is my first one! Are you going?"

"Yeah I was wondering if we could maybe take a picture together at the dance? Maybe I could get your number"

Yeah of course we can here is my number!

"Sweet thanks I am looking forward to the dance"

All of a sudden the bell rang, we spent the whole mod talking and I did not study at all but who cares Brad asked for my number! I debated about texting him all day at school but I thought I probably should not, maybe I should wait till he texts me first.

I went home and waited all night for him to text me but he never did. Maybe I over-thought it? Maybe he just wanted to be nice? *Phone dings* Oh my gosh this could be him! I read the text "Hey it is Brad just thought I would text you so you had my number ;)". Oh my gosh this is insane I must tell someone. Maybe I will call one of my friends who I'm going to the dance with! It is getting late though I guess I will just tell them in the morning.

The next morning, I woke up to a good morning text from— you guessed it, Brad. This is so unexpected I do not know what to do. How do I act at school? I feel like a celebrity. The most popular kid in school is texting me.

I walk into school and see Kiley running out of school crying— tears are all down her face, and her mascara is everywhere. I wonder what happened. Then she comes up to me and yells, "You, this is all your fault. I knew there was something about you I did not like and I could not figure it out until now. If you thought your life was miserable before just wait, you have no idea what is coming. Have fun with my leftovers." Kiley screamed so the whole hallway could hear. I had no idea what the heck she was talking about. All I could wonder is if it had something to do with Brad. No way they would have anything to do with each other though right?

Later that day I get a text from Brad "Hey meet in the library for lunch? We need to talk." I responded and wondered what he could have possibly wanted to talk about. Now things are starting to make sense though. So much is happening on this Tuesday and the homecoming dance is this Saturday. This is going to be one long week.

The bell rings and I head to the library. Sure enough Brad is sitting at the table we sit at every time. He starts being super flirty with me. I finally just asked him. Hey Brad, I have a question. Kiley came up to me crying and saying something like this is all my fault. Do you know what she is talking about by chance?

"Uh yeah I do actually so Kiley and I have been dating for 3 years and we were very happy too but then I saw you and I noticed you since you first walked into the school from a far. Once I saw you in the library I thought about coming up to you multiple times but I was so nervous. Then I thought to myself well I cannot do this to Kiley it is not fair to her. But then I thought to myself the more I see you and get to know you the more I realize how nice you are and sweet and well Kiley is the opposite."

"Well yeah I noticed she was not nice to me from the second I got here and I never knew what I did to her but right from the start she tried to get everyone to turn against me so it was really hard to make friends."

"Yeah she can be tough sometimes if I knew that about you and her I would have said something I am so sorry May. Basically I realized I was never happy with her. I only pretended to be. I only saw the good in her and I basically just made up—pretending she was a nice person. I realized I did not want to spend the rest of my highschool years being miserable and faking my love to her. I realized the only time I could actually be myself is when I was with you here. So that is why I texted you last night and that is also why I broke up with Kiley last night".

Okay but I still do not understand why she came up to me in the hall this morning. I do not want to be the reason you guys broke up nor do I think I am the reason you guys broke up so I am just confused.

"She asked me if there was someone else in my life and that is why all of a sudden I broke up with her. Then I told her how ever since I saw you I could picture myself with you more than her and I just did not want to just keep stringing her along having her think this relationship is working when I clearly do not have feelings for her like I used to. Look I know we just met and all, May but I really think I could like you. I want to stay being your friend. I hope you do not think I am coming on too strong or anything but I cannot keep my feelings inside any longer."

"Look Brad this is really sweet and all—you are really nice but I really am not here to create enemies with anyone. Maybe in the future we can be something but for right now I would really just want to be your friend. I hope you do not have hard feelings towards me Brad I really do want to be your friend!"

"It is okay, May I totally get it, who knows, maybe Kiley will forgive both of us now" (Brad said laughing).

The next day I tried to find Kiley and see if she would want to start over. Sure enough she did, she was acting really weird towards me but who cares I am just glad I can start over with her.

"Kiley, what the heck I thought you hated May, why are you going to be friends with her now I am so confused" (Kiley's friend Margaret questioned).

"Relax Margaret, I have a plan. I am going to convince her we are friends now and then I am going to get Brad Jealous. May and Brad will start dating by winter. I have no doubt about it then once

I know they are locked in. I will come in for the kill and have Brad cheat on her with me. Sweet little May will have no idea what just hit her" (Kiley laughed).

"Kiley you are truly evil and I love it" (Both Kiley and Margaret walked away laughing).

Sure enough Kiley was right by winter May and Brad were inseparable. Everything was falling into play with Kiley's plan. May and Kiley were friends. Everyone loved May now and May and Brad were as happy as ever.

After Winter Break Margaret went up to Kiley "Kiley when is this happening I cannot wait any longer to see little May cry her eyes out. She is so dumb to think Brad still does not have feelings for you still."

"Margaret these things take time, here is what I am thinking. Mike is throwing a party Friday. We have to convince May to go. She goes, we go, Brad goes. You distract May get her away from Brad. I will go up to Brad flirt with him until he cannot resist any longer but to kiss me. May will see and go home crying her sweet eyes out" (Kiley explained).

"May—hey girl, listen Margaret and I are going to a party Friday at Mike's house and you need to come out with us. It will be a lot of fun!" (Kiley convinced May to go out).

Friday night came and everything was planned, everyone was going out and Kiley had her plan to get revenge on May and get back together with Brad.

We all went to the party and I am excited this is my first high school party! I had my doubts but what could go wrong. I am with my friends and my boyfriend is here somewhere. Speaking of, I should probably go find him.

"May hey I have been looking for you"

Oh hey Margaret I was actually looking for Brad. Have you seen him?

"Oh yeah I saw him over by the punch I think he was talking with Kiley"

I look over and there he is with her. Oh my gosh my heart just shattered into a million pieces. Brad is over there making out with his ex-girlfriend. My emotions were all over the place. Do I go over there or do I leave? The one thing I cannot do is cry. I decided to call my mom to pick me up. Luckily it was still early and she was awake. She asked if I wanted to talk but I told her I wanted to be alone. I received many missed calls from Brad and many text messages.

I could not get myself to call him back, maybe in the future but for now I cannot call him, I cannot look at him, I cannot even think about him. Goodbye Brad.

3

Hiraeth

Danielle Chan

Taipei - Taiwan

February 2, 1943

The letter the telegram boy brings is ripped at the sides, its edges fraying, but I recognize Hunter's handwriting sprawled across the parchment paper.

Dear Everly,

The night sky is beautiful. I like the world like this: Serene. Contained. Quiet.

The tranquility makes me remember when we moved to the prairies so we could get a clearer view of the stars. Right now, as colors have yet to permeate the heaven, I can see them clearly. Some are blue. Some silver. Some white.

Twinkling, winking, smiling, flashing.

I remember when I was an orphan. The world I thought I knew was merely a constant change. Nothing stayed. No one stayed.

But you gave me a home.

Do you remember when we built our cottage?

I remember how I carved the crib for our daughter and you painted it so beautifully with white and hints of butter-yellow. The bright, mellow colored yellow that is the exact shade of when the sun sets and the fields darken — but not so much that the beauty is completely withdrawn or faded.

Everly, you filled our home with warmth and love.

You made me feel as though I truly belonged in a place; that I was.

You were the chink of light in my tunnel of darkness; the rose in my field of dying flowers.

I think of home right now, and I remember how happy we were.

Home was my heaven. My paradise. My own Elysium.

Oh, Everly, I long for home. I miss you.

Hunter

March 5, 1943

Our daughter plays amongst the meadows, her chubby feet bringing her to explore every corner of her tiny world. She laughs, running past the open door and clutching my arm. I smile. She runs back outside, nearly tripping over her tiny legs.

The sun is setting, the lake shimmering.

The mountain-tops are drizzled with flecks of amber and orange and yellow.

The leaves that lie on the soft carpet of Earth and soil have withered away. Shrunk. Decayed.

So right and yet so wrong.

I watch as the world is immersed once again in golden light. The iridescent shades of the pink and red and peach growing dimmer and dimmer, shyer and shyer, fading until gradually there's no more.

Somewhere far away I know Hunter is watching the same sunset as I am.

I reach out and unfold the new letter I received today.

Dear Everly,

I remember the happiest day of my life- when you agreed to marry me.

At that moment, how could I describe the infinite amount of emotions I was feeling? How many could my heart hold?

But now, with the war, I see the world as it truly is.

The world is dark. The world is cruel and atrocious and full of war and battle. The world is engulfed in greed and jealousy and hatred.

I wish I could come home. You gave me my dream and I grasped it. I cherished it. I treasured it. I had a direction; a purpose to serve.

But now I am lost in this Hell, lost in a littered graveyard of former beauty, painted with rivers of scarlet red.

I long to come home. I dream of walking down the battered pathway and knocking once more on the wooden doorway – then to step into our cottage again. To feel the smooth wooden planks under my bare feet. To feel the silk of your hand-sewn draperies slide through the gaps of my fingers and know that – for once – I am safe.

Everly, I hope and wish and dream and remember.

But I must thank you for something.

For making my dark world light again.

For being the star that guided me when I was lost.

And for loving me.

The world is ever so beautiful with love. Love and hope and dreams are what shape the beauty in our universe.

I would do anything to come home. These thoughts agonize and burrow through my mind day and night. I wake up and go to bed longing and yearning for home. I see our old photograph – yellowing, curling, its ink fading – and I long for when my life was still carefree.

I miss you so much I feel like my heart will burst.

Hunter

April 10, 1943

As I open the front door, I am met with someone unfamiliar, a soldier dressed in uniform. He is youthful, boyish, but in his eyes linger sadness.

He bows, his voice shaking as he says, "I'm so sorry, Miss."

"Pardon me?"

"Hunter . . ." I can see his hands clenching and unclenching, struggling to hold on to whatever strength he has left that has not been stolen from him. "He would have wanted you to have this."

My eyes meet his, and a tiny crack forms in my heart. His eyes, defeated, whisper, *"I'm sorry. I'm so, so sorry."*

I squeeze my eyes shut and lean, trembling, against the unyielding wall.

Dead, lifeless, lying somewhere amongst the blood-stained prairies, his heart no longer ablaze.

The crack within my heart breaks, forming an endless void that burrows deep within me. "Thank you," I say to the soldier. "I'm sorry, too."

He tips his hat, gives me a small smile, and leaves.

Heavenly Father,

I head out tomorrow at dawn. This mission will be dangerous, but Sergeant Robertson promises rewards. I am doing this in hopes that I will finally be permitted to travel home.

I love Everly. I have never loved anyone as I love her.

Everything I do is for Everly.

It will always, always be for her.

I would risk my life in hopes that she has the chance to live a normal life.

But isn't that what we all look for? A chance, just a simple glimmer of hope, that we can live our dreams for a single second?

I would do it again, and again, and again. No matter how long it takes.

So if I make it, if I am granted the permission to go back home, I would show her the world. And Everly deserves the world. She deserves to see the beauty of even the smallest things. The way the trees sway lightly to the breeze; the feel of the wind tickling her cheeks; the tiny dew drops that form in the wee hours of the morning. I'd get to watch the stars with her again, watch as the constellations form and, together, paint a picture.

Tonight the sky is clear again. The world is quiet.

There are no battles. No wars.

The stars are infinite, stretching across the vast boundaries of the sky. And it is beautiful, like this.

Dear Heavenly Father,

I look up, and I see our daughter sitting outside on the fields, her eyes wide and fascinated with the twinkling lights above her. She reaches up, trying to finger the stars, gasping when one streaks across the sky.

"Mama," she cries. "Mama! Stars!"

Her eyes, full of light, turn towards me, and I can see Hunter inside of them. His smile, the way his eyes gleamed when he was happy. The corners of my mouth turn up and I walk outside to sit with her.

Our daughter crawls on my lap and, slowly, falls asleep in my arms. I look down at the letter, reading the last line as she sighs in her sleep, smiling as she ventures deep into her dreams.

"Oh, Hunter," I whisper, looking up. "I am, I am."

I hope Everly is watching the stars tonight.

4

I Never Wear White

Mel Buckingham

Milford, Connecticut - United States

James picks me up from the airport. I cling to the remains of our fragile friendship like a lifeline, like a rope pulling me out of a canyon. It's gotten frayed over the years, though worn. I'm amazed it still holds my weight.

I changed my flights for him. He's only in town for a night, so I made sure I'd be there in time. I don't tell him this, of course. I can't make it appear as though I care more than he does, though we both know I do. We politely pretend like I've moved on, the way I should have years ago. I visit my hometown sometimes, see all my old friends, drive by my old house. I pretend like I'm not spending thousands of dollars on plane tickets just to see an old flame I never let burn out.

He's waiting by his Range Rover, trunk already open. I remember sitting in the passenger's seat and looking at him; his profile is burned into my brain. I remember kissing in this car, hands on a khaki-clad thigh, tugging at a plaid skirt. Seventeen was so long ago. Just five years, but a lifetime and a half.

He liked me in white. Said it once in passing, at a party. I was in high-waisted jeans, he'd hook his fingers into the belt loops and pull me in, arms around my waist, skin exposed by my white top. Neckline low, pronouncing the hollows of my collarbones, the length of my neck. His chapped lips brushing down the side of it. I shivered and he rubbed his hand over my arm.

"You cold?" he asked. I'm always cold. It was December in Tennessee and I was pink in the face from the alcohol, and trembling from the cold.

"You look nice," he said. A small smile, but the eyes crinkled. That's how you know it's real.

"You look pretty in white," he said, shifting from foot to foot. It's polyester and nylon, that shirt—if you can call it that. Flimsy piece of fabric that I stole from some fast fashion outlet I can't remember. I quit shoplifting because of him. Quit smoking too.

He dressed well. Cotton blends. Cashmere, wool. Thick denim. Muted colors: blue, beige, black. The occasional adventurous article. My favorite was a linen button-down in a pale pink, sleeves rolled up to his elbows. I only saw him wear it once. Did I tell him I liked it?

He liked me in white. He told me that. Did I ever tell him?

I like you in pink. I like you in linen. I like you in your overpriced jeans, your button-down shirt, in my room, in my arms.

Maybe he got scared. Maybe bored, or tired, or in over his head. Maybe he pictured me in white, walking towards him with a smile on my face, and realized he didn't like it so much after all.

I change in the airport bathroom before walking out—black jeans, small top. Splash on some perfume, ruffle up my hair. Nothing to make him think I put in any effort for him, but knowing I did.

I take a deep breath before I look at him. He's a little bit taller, his shoulders broader. He's wearing a short-sleeved button-down with pineapples on it. Pineapples.

"Hey," he says, with a smile.

"Hey," I reply. I hug with both arms; he hugs back with one. We chat in the car—how are you doing, how have you been, what's new—nothing gets said. The sun's just going down. He smells good, vetiver and amber.

We go out for pizza, he leaves an extra chair in between us. The guy behind the counter recognizes us—we used to come here all the time. We sit, we talk, we eat. He smiles, his eyes crinkling, and it flattens me like a truck. I stare at him. Overpriced jeans. Black sneakers. Pineapples.

"Nice shirt," I say. He grins.

"Thanks, it's a new favorite."

"Why pineapples?" I ask.

He shrugs.

"Thought it was fun."

You used to think I was fun, I want to say. Too much fun, actually. Not the kind of girl you want to stay with long-term. He was a safe, dependable type. Jeans and a blue shirt type. Not really a pineapple shirt kind of guy. I want to run my fingers down the buttons, flip the collar up and down, feel his forearms around me. I want to see it wrinkled and inside out, and on my floor. Is this how he dresses now? Is it for me? Is he making a point?

James laughs at my jokes. He always thought I was funny. We get our usual order, and I watch him save the crusts for last like he always does. He offers to grab me a refill for my drink. I watch him walk away with my stomach in my throat.

He drives me to my cousin's house, helps me with my suitcase. We stand by his car, and I wonder when I'm going to see him again.

"Thanks," I say, as he sets my suitcase down.

"No problem," he replies. The air is hot and humid, July in Nashville, and I still feel shivers down my arms.

A year? Two? Five? Ten? I wonder what he'll look like. I wonder what he'll be wearing. I'm smiling so hard. The second I stop, I'll cry.

"I'm glad I got to see you," I say. I look at one of the pineapples on his right shoulder instead of meeting his eyes.

"Yeah, me too," he says. Hugs with both arms this time. I flatten my palms against his back, then bunch the back of his shirt in my fingers. My chin on his shoulders, I breathe him in, wondering how long I can hold my breath.

We say goodbye. I walk into the house, greet my cousin, go to the guest room. I take off my shirt and fold it delicately. My hands are shaking so badly it takes me ten minutes. I press my face to it, then put it in a plastic bag, and tie it tightly. I tell myself I'm crazy, then put the bag in the outside pocket of my suitcase. I fall asleep in an oversized t-shirt, and dream of myself in white.

The next day, my cousin and I go grocery shopping. She gets her daughter's favorite cereal. I buy a pineapple.

5

Island Boy

Leonie Milde

Isle of Raasay - United Kingdom

"You know you don't need to leave." You say, loading the last of my boxes into the boot of my car. It's been a week and you haven't stopped reminding me that this isn't on you. If I told you the whole story, you wouldn't even have come down to say goodbye.

Tiny, fleecy lambs are bleating for their mothers down by the shore to announce spring. We met in spring. I was scared of the calves and you took my hand to show me how to stroke their plushy fringes. They didn't teach me that in the city. My Disney princess view on farming, you call it.

"I'm not right for you." But that isn't the truth. I am exactly right for you. My head fits perfectly on your shoulder when we're huddled around the fire overlooking the ocean, Skye sitting in the distance in all its glory, the afternoon sun illuminating the mountains the way it only glows this far north and deep into December. The tweed blanket your grandfather gave you as a wee boy is just big enough to cover the both of us and our little wool cocoon is anything if not exactly right.

I always thought love would be easier. More straightforward. I guess maybe because for a long while, it was. It was exciting and adventurous, ticking cities and countries off our bucket list, writing late at night with my feet in your lap and the dog sprawled across the couch like paint splatter, reading passages out loud and watching your eyes light up when you recognised yourself in my characters. Like the way you tilt your head when you don't know what I'm talking about or press your lips together when I'm ranting about something irrelevant so you wait it out but you never look at me with anything other than admiration. All my characters tilt their heads.

You know I know I am right for you, too. Our compatibility was never questioned. So you don't comment on this. You make no attempts at a goodbye, either, avoiding my eyes but scanning the lines of my face as if to memorise them, to recall when you find dog hair in our bed tonight, smell me on your pillow.It's terrible to think of just how well we worked together, my words and your drawings, your cameras and my beautiful dog, my hand and yours as we wade through the muddy heather behind our house.

"You promised we'd break up on good terms." You say.

This is a promise I made years ago, before we ever met, after months of texting and calling, pandemic restrictions keeping us apart, the anticipation of our eventual encounter a steady gas leak, one spark away from everything we could become. And did.

When we met up, it felt like a reunion. Like of course you are here at the same time as me and hug me so tightly I can hear your heart beat through your winter coat. Of course I look up and recognise every inch of your face from hours of video calls and you lean down to kiss me without hesitating and your stubble feels so familiar under my palms because for weeks, I've laid awake thinking of this exact moment.

"We are breaking up on good terms." I insist. "I just hope we never speak again because I don't want someone else to take my place."

"No."

I stop you with a wave of my hand. "Of course someone else is going to move into that perfect house you built for us. The forest dream cabin isn't a bachelor pad. The little book nook demands to be shared because no bookshelf wants to house nothing but nerdy history books and catalogues of Arctic vehicles. Someone's going to fill it with children and you'll take them down to the sea and throw pebbles into the water and on a winter day, when the sun barely rises over the mountains, just for a second, you'll wait for the dog to go running after them, turning around when she's halfway there because she always, always forgets just how cold the water gets. And you'll be so happy that you got it all. That you had me and that I left."

You don't look at me while you picture this. It's going to happen because it's the way things go on the island and you love the island too much to let it die out with your generation. You have spent too many hours reading its history to me in bed, my head on your chest, to give up on it now for something as plain as a girl.

"I want you more than children."

You've said this before but never meant it. I humoured you at times but deep down I always knew I wouldn't deliver and I always told you so. Children mean permanence. Children mean staying in one place, they need stability. You can't raise children in two countries divided by four more countries. I have my dog and one day she is going to leave me and for the rest of my time, I will be half a person. But I will be half a person all over the world and I'm not willing to trade that for the perpetual fear of being a parent. My heart beating outside my body. You once told me that yours beats for me but the idea of it beating for a mini you comforts me, reassures me that I am making the right decision.

I remember the first time I realised you were meant to be a dad. We hadn't known each other very long but sitting on a car-print rug with you and your baby nephew, the utter tirelessness with which you entertained this child, I couldn't think of a better man to be a father and when the tears came, the first time you'd seen me cry, I had to tell you that I was angry at the universe because I wouldn't get to be their mother.

We lean against the boot of my car, so close we're almost touching but I'm worried that if we do, I won't go because I'm not leaving because I don't want to be with you. I'm leaving because I'm a woman of reason and it's time. This grand adventure of ours has come to an end and I need to go home, wherever that is. We are quiet because it's all been said and done. We've yelled and cried and held each other so close we were sure that when we woke up, we'd be one and none of this would be happening. I wonder if your parents are looking out the window to watch me drive away and caught this instead. The silence.

"We can move somewhere else." You tried one last time but it was never about that.

"This is your home."

"You are my home."

For a long time, we were each other's homes. Living in a van will do that to you. Waking up in new places every day will do that to you. But you always had another home and I was always just there because I was with you. I was always *his girlfriend* and never *me*. No one said the girl who wrote the novel about the island. The girl who always carries a porcelain mug with tea on her morning walk, even in the pouring rain. No, his girlfriend. The girl with the beautiful dog, sometimes. Very unusual colours.

"Will you ever tell me what this is really about?"

"I told you, I can't live in the middle of nowhere forever."

You understand but you don't believe me.

"The island will never be the same without you."

"It will be better. It will be louder."

"Why can't you stay another year? Or five?"

"Because you don't want to start over when you're 40 and have to settle for someone based on nothing but your joined wish for a child. You're young and—" I almost say handsome but your ego doesn't need it. You're beautiful. Even though your front teeth are implants because someone knocked them out with a rudder and on the way inside, you slipped on ice and dislocated both your arms. It was too stormy for a helicopter that day, the ferry wasn't running anymore, so your mum put you to bed, dislocated arms dangling next to you, until you could be airlifted to Inverness the next morning. These kinds of things don't happen to you in a city. If I'm honest, I can't wait to not worry whether I will die an entirely preventable death just because it's a bit windy that day. I also can't wait to not care how long you're out for a walk because as soon as it's five minutes longer than you predicted, I am back on that Orkney cliff, wrapped in a neon yellow Coast Guard coat, waiting for yet another helicopter to retrieve you from the bottom of it. And the months on crutches that followed your titanium hip implantation. 'Main character shit', you called it, but I was terrified and nothing else.

"And?"

More things I don't say: caring, polite, my mother loves you more than me. You are creative and ambitious, windproof and you never tire of complimenting me. "You have money." I say instead. "You're a catch."

"But it's not enough to make you stay."

You look too sad, wondering why I'm not sadder. I hold the key in the palm of my hand. Four words and you'd despise me forever, I could break your heart, snatch it clean in two, when you find out it has all been a lie. "This was never meant to be a forever thing."

"Says who?"

"Logic? The 28-hour drive from my family to yours?"

"You don't even like your family."

Touché.

I'll miss the island, too. I'll miss the tranquility and the fact no one ever locks their doors. Knowing that when my dog runs away, the neighbour will send her right back to me and people drive so carefully to avoid sheep that she can comfortable trot on the main road without a lead. The people's respect for nature, their faithfulness to their home and the holiness of Sabbath, still so prevalent that nobody would dare hang their washing outside on a Sunday, even if it's windy and sunny, the perfect combination to dry your bedsheets, even in the depth of winter. I'll miss learning facts like this. You don't learn about real life in the city. But the island doesn't need us. It's been here long before us and perhaps the villagers won't even notice our absence because we were never more than Austrian intruders to begin with.

I'll miss dancing. The dog doesn't dance with me. When I get up and ask Alexa to play German rock, she rolls over on her back as if she could shield her ears from the morning disturbance and no matter how much I chant and jump, slap my thighs and try to lure her down with words like food, walks and snack, she barely lifts an eyebrow. Every morning, my next step is to turn to you and stretch out my hand, careful not to grab yours because you're stronger than me and could easily pull me back, bury me under the warmth of your body and then that's it for my plans to get an early start to my day. Most days, you watch me, the dog snoozes while you are mesmerised by my legs until you can't resist the urge to touch me, the teasing hand lingering only inches away from yours, and you get out of bed, wrap me in an embrace with one swift motion and the dog is too jealous to stay where she is. And then we dance. To music you don't understand, that's too loud for the dog's liking, but for me you both twirl and shake until we're out of breath, collapsing on top of the bed. You won't admit it, but those always turn out to be the best days.

But I miss home. Your friends are like family and mine are people we visited twice a year, like a chore. Every once in a while, I flew back by myself and missed the dog and third wheeled my friends' relationships. We grew up together but grew apart while I was gone because there are some things you can't share over FaceTime. You have to discuss them over brunch, over mimosas and avocado toast on the busy sidewalk outside Le Pain Quotidien, the concrete sizzling in the July sun. It never gets hot on the island. Most days it's grey and cold yet just one beautiful afternoon will make you forget about all of this in the blink of an eye. And then it's paradise and you can't imagine living anywhere else ever. And I can't. Maybe because I don't want to. Because when the power is out or the wifi hasn't worked in a day there is nothing to do but cuddle and walk and when it's too windy for the ferry to come in, there's no mail or milk and it's easy to forget that just a few years ago I was living in a city with 8.4 million people.

The Isle of Raasay is about the same size and shape as Manhattan but only 161 people live on it. 162, until now, though I never registered. I always wanted to, wanted your last name, but you never asked and it would have just meant more paperwork back then and again now. Maybe you regret it in this very moment, that it's so easy for me to leave, that we don't need to reunite a year from now in a lawyer's office and sign papers. Maybe it will be easier this way, knowing we never actually belonged to another. In the eyes of the government.

It's too sunny for this. Sunny days are for early starts and picnics, for 2-hour lunch breaks and calling it work because you took a photo of a whisky bottle before lying down in the grass next to me and trying to identify birds by their songs, watching the ferry come in with curious tourists hopping over from Skye for a taste of further remoteness, to take a photo or two and get the evening ferry back. You love ferries, with the innocence of a young child. Island life does that to you. When there has been no evidence of an outside world for days, aside from the internet, the ferry is a welcome friend whose return radiates comfort and assurance. Not that the shop, which looks like someone's living room with a clear fridge, has ever run out of anything at all no matter the weather, but it's nice to know that if you want to, you can leave. Except better weather means you don't want to. It is too magical. It is exactly what people picture. A romanticised version of life except tougher and muddier and colder. But it is all pretend.

For 4 years, we have been pretending. At first, we pretended we weren't in a pandemic, pretended that we knew each other beyond FaceTime and selfies and our social media facades. When we finally met, we pretended we'd known each other forever and dove right into a state of utter comfort, of familiarity and habit. We pretended I was an island girl like you were an island boy, like I didn't have a life 28 hours and two ferries south before I'd moved up north to be by the beach for a few months while the world recovered. Like I hadn't downloaded tinder for a socially distanced walk on another island every once in a while only to end up with this intriguing, aggressively-interested-in-everything-person two islands away in the middle of a nationwide tier 4 lockdown with no chance of meeting any time soon. We pretended I was ok in the head until one day I was. Because your touch didn't make me flinch like all the other men before you. We pretended it was fate. And we pretended it was ok.

"You said we're a family."

Oh, we could have been.

"Petal and I are a family. You and Sarah will be a family."

"I don't want Sarah, I've spoken to her twice."

"I think you'll be great together."

"I want you."

"You can't have me."

"Why?"

I guess it's inevitable. Maybe it always was. Can't keep a secret like this forever. You are growing impatient as I contemplate this revelation, this final heartbreak I'd hoped to spare you but the only thing that will set me free.

"I had an abortion."

You look disappointed yet unsurprised. Hurt, but not angry. "When?"

"Last month, when I went to Glasgow to 'visit Katie'." I did visit Katie. She held my hand.

"Why didn't you talk to me?"

"I knew what you'd say."

"It wasn't your place to assume."

"It wasn't yours to decide."

You curl your hand into a fist and uses it to slam the boot shut, just a little harder than necessary. "You don't know what I would have said."

"I'm not 15 anymore, Alastair. A grown woman with a job and a house and a partner who'd have made the best father? Who'd have dropped everything? That's not the situation that justifies abortions."

"So you did it in secret instead?"

I tried to tell you, when I first found out. Because I was used to you being the first one I told anything but the initial gush of vomit that the second pink line caused didn't put me in the mood to discuss it and soon I learned that it was easier to just never bring it up.

"How long did you wait?"

"Six weeks."

You run your hands through your hair, desperately repeating '6 weeks' to yourself, walking in a little circle, the gravel of the driveway crunching under your boots. "So essentially the last 3 months were a lie?"

I can't argue with that, though I want to. I want to tell you that every night I fell asleep next to you, I meant it. That I was lying awake thinking about the pastoral childhood we could give this child, how much the dog would love it, the primary school who currently had two students plus one from the nursery in the same classroom. The fact that 161 people would look after this child. The fact that I did not want it. I want to tell you that I planned out the surprise announcement, a cheesy t-shirt that said Best Dad, or subtly leave the test on your nightstand and watch your face ache in confusion and light up with joy. But I didn't. Because the cynical woman you fell in love with, the one who never believed that two people were meant to spend their whole lives together despite Emily Blunt and John Krasinski existing, she had an exit strategy. She's had one since she was 16 and it never changed and she hoped it would never come to it but there was no decision to be made. I was not going to be a mother.

I didn't decide right away that I would leave you after the appointment. For a few more weeks, I told myself I could stay another year or two, early thirties are a great time for a man to find someone new. Someone who's done traveling, confident in her career, ready to settle down and single-handedly repopulate the island with you. And you'll forget. Maybe not about me, maybe not about that winter snowed in at a Swiss mountain lodge that resulted in a 300-page illustrated book and the dog learning every trick imaginable, the fire cracking because it hadn't dried enough, a cabin that could only be reached by skis and neither of us could ski. Maybe not about the fact that while you put the house together beam by beam, I made you sandwiches and chased the dog away from the nail gun. Maybe you'll repaint the kitchen because when we did it together, I played trashy music and we scrubbed the paint of each other's faces over the sink and our laughter melted into every paint-stroke. Or you'll repaint it simply because it's the colour of my eyes.

"I didn't lie."

"You deliberately withheld crucial information from me, I think it's safe to say you lied."

"I didn't want to hurt you."

You contemplate this with a deep, angry sigh and I wish you'd scream. I wish you'd shake me, ask me why after all this time I am still playing games. Wasn't it enough when I slept with the vet right after we got together? Hoping you'd leave me because I was afraid of attachment, commitment, closeness in every sense of the word but I was glued to you and it terrified me? Wasn't it enough that I went back to Vienna for six months hoping you'd find someone better so I wouldn't have to admit that I couldn't stop fantasising about living on this stupid island with you? Wasn't it enough that I came back and I stayed and we swam with otters on the coldest day of the year and I never complained that this life felt like someone else's? Like we were just going through the motions. Weren't you enough? Weren't we?

"You're a bitch." You say dryly and I deserve it.

And now here we stand on this island of your heart, of my choosing, and you have chosen it over me. I have chosen it for you. Over me. And it shouldn't be this hard to go back to civilisation, in driving distance of a supermarket, with cafés and restaurants, museums and winter sunsets after 3 pm. I am so close to being freed from this cage I have built for myself, telling myself I can't do all these things I dreamed of in my youth, summers in the north of Sweden, winters in the mountains. I am a twenty minute ferry ride away from another island, which is only a small bridge away from the island that is Great Britain and then, 35 minutes under the English channel, the mainland will be waiting for me. I will cross borders and detect them only by the signs on the side of the highway, barely noticeable. France, Belgium, Luxemburg, Germany, finally, Austria. I will desert these ancient chapels, monasteries in ruins, abandoned medieval castles, for horse-drawn carriages in the city centre, baroque palaces, well-groomed and swamped with tourists in tulle skirts and sneakers. Vienna is white and bright. My life, once an ad for outdoor gear and functional apparel in our very own enchanted forest, will be a different kind of fairytale, one without a prince.

"We had a good run." I pat his shoulder as I turn away, swiftly, like condoling a goalie after letting a ball run through their fingers during a soccer match. Better luck next time.

I load the dog into the passenger seat and buckle her seatbelt. She doesn't know. She's been strapped in this harness so many times before, for adventures across the continent, and each time we returned to her fluffy bed in front of the floor to ceiling windows with a perfect view of the squirrels helping themselves to the bird feeders, to greet the seals basking in the sunshine just down the road if someone left the kitchen door open by accident. She'll have to adjust to city life again, until we move wherever we're moving next. The parks, the roads, the children screaming and running. She doesn't know yet.

"Stay." You say despite everything, opening the driver's side door for me, holding it as I get in.

You look taller from below. Even though you're barely taller than me when I'm standing, I now feel intimidated by you as you tower over me. I want to tell you that we were never meant to last. That after all this time, I still stalk your ex on instagram, counting the days until our relationship has lasted longer than yours because the exhilaration of your love was only matched by the fatigue of being all this. An island girl.

The electric engine makes no noise and I can hear your bare feet on the pebbles as you walk back up the road to a home we built that was never mine to begin with.

6

Lover's Reunion

Micah Brocker

Seattle, Washington - United States

Reality is much different than the dream you keep in your head. And sadly, for me, reality has never surpassed my imaginary creations of love I tend to each night before my eyes slip to sleep.

If it did, he would be home.

Any second now.

I visualize wrapping myself around him. I can't fall asleep. Not when he's late, not even when I know I must be up early, not for the life of me, because he will be here soon. At least that's what I tell myself.

I imagine him smothering me in hugs and kisses, whispering that he never wants to leave me again. My clothes are off as I wait with anticipation in bed for his arrival.

He is going rush to bed with a sweet grin, finding me naked, he'll enfold me in his muscular arms, and we'll whisper against the night until the sun rises.

But he didn't come at eleven, when his flight was supposed to. Nor at 12. And not even at 1. My eyes slip closed like concrete. My alarm will wake me up in four hours.

The sound of luggage dragging upstairs, and a door slamming reinvigorated my exhausted brain at almost 2. He is home. I grin even though my head pounds from sleep deprivation.

The bedroom door doesn't open. My arms don't wrap around him, and his body doesn't rest on mine.

Instead, I hear the fridge open, and a low rumble of a voice that is not satisfied.

I wait, fighting my eyelids to keep my anticipation. I last 20 minutes before I can no longer handle the waiting. I slip on my robe and pad down the stairs to see him in the living room. My eyes can't open fully in the lit room. He is fuzzy, and after missing him for too long I want to see him clearly. I strain my eyelids past the pain to glimpse his face.

A fuzzy handsome man. My fuzzy handsome man.

I want to kiss him, but his mouth fills with salmon dip he scoops with a chip from a hand that doesn't hold me as I worm my wait to his lap.

I settle for kissing the top of his hair.

He won't look up at me as I try to recreate my dreams.

"My car got towed." he says accusingly.

Shit. My sleepy brain churns. Hadn't I seen his car out front? I think, but everything is blurry. When was that?

"Shoot, I swear I just saw it," I say.

He told me to wipe it off while he was gone. I told him to text me any instructions.

He never texted, and well, I forgot about the chore.

"Going to be expensive." He gripes.

"I'm sorry," I say. And I am. I didn't mean for his car to get towed. I wish he had never gone, because I bet it would have gotten towed even if he was home. I don't say this.

"The parade!" I exclaim, my sleep stupor finally clearing long enough to let a solution through, "I bet they cleared the road of cars for the parade on Saturday."

"Were there no parking signs?"

I squint over his head. I don't remember any parking signs, but I also couldn't say there wasn't. My brain pulses. I wish this hadn't happened.

"I don't think so," I answer.

"If there weren't signs, then my car had a ticket two days prior to the parade." He illuminates my negligence: there could have been a ticket on his vehicle for perhaps half the week and I had done nothing.

I did remember walking by and seeing some sort of square on his windshield, but filth covered the car, and I couldn't be certain. I'd been finishing a run, and I'd said to myself, "Oh I'll be back out to check that." But I didn't. I never came back. Honestly, I'm not sure what I would have done if I had come back out. I can't drive stick. There is a good possibility I couldn't have moved it even if I had known it was to be done.

None of this is the issue, or something I can say. His face is tight and red, my handsome fuzzy man is crystal clear now, and he is a raging bull. Our reunion is rotting in reality. The dream of a perfect reunion has withered. All because an airline employee told him the wrong baggage claim number, and his flight was delayed, and his car is towed, and he hasn't given me a single kiss.

I wish I'd stayed upstairs. Tucked in comfortably with candied ignorance.

My stomach plummets as he begins listing the rest of my offenses. The water for the plants is low. My cat is scratching the couch. I couldn't pick him up at the airport because I don't drive stick. His car is going to cost an arm and a leg.

I want to cry.

My dreams were much sweeter. I love that dream more than this stark reality. Yelling in the kitchen at 2 AM, while my eyes burn to hide my sorrow from him.

"Leave," I want to say, "so I can keep loving you."

Micah Brocker

7

The Orange Grove

Rose McCoy

Morgantown, West Virginia - United States

By the time I saw him again, the change between us was like a rift, as visible as anything intangible can be, as palpable as the mistake that had caused it. It was fine when his ship rolled in. It was fine when it docked. It was still fine when he strode towards me—the picture-perfect moment laid out before us, of the man gone off to war and his delicate wife waiting as they met once again—but when he approached me and removed his cap, he looked at me with the saddest, most rejected eyes you've ever seen and said, soft as anything: "I know what you did."

My breath hitched. It would be years before the image of the conniving young dame grew mainstream, of the housewife so pleasing in dress and demeanor even as the cogs of her mind whirred to life in secret, sly deceit, and yet the image was not far from me at all—if she wasn't popular in the culture yet, I was as good a representative as any. So even as my husband said this—those five words so heavy and desperate, which I knew quite well the meaning behind—I could do nothing but pretend.

Ever the actor was I, indeed. I said, "I'm sorry?"—innocent of face and slight of frame, thankful for the veil which hid my eyes (and hoping, still, that they didn't express as much as his had upon his initial announcement).

Hearing the words, my husband's face darkened. He clutched my forearms and pulled me close, not for an embrace but rather a harsh and forceful whisper in my ear. "Don't do this, Marie. Just don't. I know what you did, and you can't fix it. You've ruined us—cut us straight to the quick." He released me and turned away. "I can't even bear to look at you."

The words stung even as I pretended not to understand them. I love my husband—anyone who says otherwise is a liar. But there are ways in which I do not love him—ways in which I never could.

He was never supposed to know that.

Trying to mask my shame with a startled, confused look, I forced my features into a frown. "Charles, stop this nonsense! I haven't seen you in months and this is the first thing you mention? Some scandal I've had no part of? It's absurd!" At this, a fresh row of lines on his face I'd never seen before seemed to deepen, so I changed tactics. Softening, I said, "Let's go home, love. We can talk this over in the morning, but right now I'd like to see you for the first time in nearly a year. Is that all right?"

A cloud passed, ever so slightly, across his face. "Fine," he said—angry but not showing it, like the gentleman he is—"But know that you can't fix it. You've really done it this time, Marie. You've really done it."

I opened my mouth, then closed it. Was the damage truly irreparable? His eyes shouted a resounding *yes.* I bowed my head, offering some kind of moment of silence for the life I'd led up to this moment; even then, it was clear that things would never be the same. "Hush, now, husband," I murmured, masking my sorrow as I slipped an arm through his. "Let's go home."

So we walked, side by side like a husband and wife should, but he might as well have never gotten on the ship that brought him back to me, so immense was the distance between us. If this was what "back" was—if this was our mighty reunion after so long of being apart—I wanted no part of it.

Of course, it was all my fault.

And as much as I wanted to, I would never be able to fix it.

~ ~ ~

We arrived at home to find Douglas, our neighbor, sitting on his porch, ale in hand. When he saw us, a bright grin split his face and he lunged to hug his old friend. Jostling Charles beneath his arm, Douglas insisted that they announce his return to the rest of the neighborhood men, and soon our tiny dining table was hosting eight of Charles' best and rowdiest friends.

I made sure everyone was comfortable, passing out beers and smiling politely at their jokes. Not wanting to leave Charles alone, I stayed at the edge of the commotion for as long as I seemed welcome before one of the men announced pointedly, "This isn't the place for a woman, but if it were, she'd be the one I'd want with me!" and I had to smile and slip out.

The first thing I noticed when I stepped outside was the moon. It was out already, watching as the sky darkened—maybe watching me as my life did the same. I wished, for a moment, that we could trade places. What would it be like if I could watch all this from far below me? If I could view my own life like a movie, unable to

affect events at all? What if the entirety of my most important relationship wasn't riding on my shoulders and my shoulders alone? I
knew it was nothing but a pipe dream.

Sighing, I swept my gaze along the sodden grass. So much
money spent—so many memories made . . . so much time and
effort put into making this house a home, yet still the woven basket
leaning forlornly against the doorframe was as empty as it had been
since we'd bought it. I'd put it there for collecting fruit and flowers;
we had both a garden and a grove of orange trees, the better part
of the company I kept while Charles was away. Reaching for its
twisted handle, an idea struck me.

Even the juiciest orange could never be enough, but at least this
was something I could do with myself, some small act of apology
I could offer in the equally small hope that we weren't changed
forever. I nodded my resolve and swept slowly through the trees,
holding my dress in one hand and the basket in the other, plucking
each orange after examining it carefully. They were plump and ripe
on their branches, which were heavy from the weight: self-destruc-
tive. Only when they were arranged in the basket with lilies and
lilac did I stop collecting; I knew it wasn't enough, but for now, it
was the best I could do.

I shed a single tear, listening to the boisterous yelling from inside and knowing things would never be the same. I stood still as
the moonlight washed over me, allowing its smoky tendrils to seep
inside my bones. Maybe they could wash away my sin; maybe they
could fix this mess I'd made.

If only I deserved it.

~ ~ ~

Ten minutes later, I hadn't moved from where I stood, but I was swimming in the silence that surrounded me. Awash in it, I could hear nothing but the low moan of the wind, which whispered condolences to me each time it passed. Everything was still and quiet and in stark contrast to what was happening inside. The soundlessness was a void that filled me top to toe.

But just then something broke it. My head whipped around to where I'd heard the rustle, but there was nothing there.

Then, equally as sudden, I heard my name.

"Who's there?" I turned in a circle, filled with apprehension. I felt the panic rise as a hand clamped across my mouth from behind, stifling the scream that would have inevitably come.

"Marie, it's me. It's Marjorie."

Relieved, I sighed heavily and the hand fell away. Closing my eyes, I felt but didn't see her as my best friend turned to face me. I imagined how she looked in the near-dark, moonlight shining in her eyes and reflecting off her pale skin, hair long and flowing over her back. She'd look at me with concern and love, mouth half open if she glanced, by chance, at mine, wringing her hands as if that could erase our sin.

"Marie," she said softly, "would you look at me?"

It occurred to me then that if Charles knew what we'd done, and there were only two perpetrators of the crime, then there was only one possible culprit of who had revealed the secret—but Marjorie must have known this, because what she said next was, "I didn't tell him, but I heard that he knows. Please look at me, Marie. Please."

I inhaled again and opened my eyes slowly, taking in the beauty of her in stages so as not to overwhelm. And what a true beauty she was—the spitting image of Charles, really, but thinner, more delicate, more intimate; as I looked at her, she fought the urge to reach for me, cupping my cheek in her palm and staring at me as if I might shatter.

"Where is he?"

"Inside."

"With his friends?"

"Yes."

She moved her hand to my heart, beating rapidly with both love and fear (though, really, aren't the two the same?).

"Are you angry?"

"Not so much as he is . . . Marjorie, how did he know?"

She sighed, as softly as the beating of a sparrow's wing. "I . . . " Her head dropped, sorrowful. "I don't know."

So I told her it was all right, because what else could I say? Hidden by the cloak of night, I clutched her body to me. Kissed her cheek as a mother would, dried her tears while keeping mine at bay. She was a bundle of softness, of kindness, of grace; a medley of the greatest parts of being a woman, and in that moment—for all it was worth—she was mine.

Our dresses rustled as she pulled back from me. "Tell my brother . . ."

But she couldn't finish, because the door abruptly, brashly pushed open, accompanied by the stomping of boots, and in a flash of white and satin she was gone.

Laughing, yelling and shoving, seven dark shapes stumbled past me, tearing the moment in two like an unwanted photograph. One lingered at the door, still wearing his uniform, so I gathered myself and came to him—perhaps we were as magnetic as we'd ever been. I could see him preparing to ask where I'd been, losing his impulse control to the drink, but when I handed him his gift, the question in his eyes was erased. It wasn't replaced with anything, no love or affection that I could see, but I was relieved not to have to deflect his accusations regardless.

That night, although it's true that alcohol and anger don't mix, he didn't hit me. I didn't expect him to, but I was prepared for it, so when he simply stripped and sunk into bed, the relief came instantly. I did the same, keeping my distance; grateful, even when I woke the next morning to the smell of sour citrus and lilac, finding the flowers crushed and oranges smashed in a Pollock painting of grief.

~ ~ ~

That afternoon, when I couldn't stand the silence anymore, I suggested that Charles and I go into town. It was a sunny Friday afternoon, so we'd likely be greeted by friends and acquaintances, and I thought it might help raise our spirits.

The car puffed into a parking spot, and already I felt better. Charles' silence didn't help me read his feelings, but I assumed they hadn't changed, probably not despite but because of the quiet. He was stony as we got out of the car, the sun hitting our faces like a slap. I led us towards the nearest boutique.

He waited by the door for me and said nothing when I emerged empty-handed; he merely clasped my arm possessively and led us forward. This went on for the better part of an hour. He said nothing even when I strode right past my favorite jewelry store, freshly reopened since the end of the war. I wondered if this was a new permanence: overeager effort on my part, and silence on his.

We dined in a formal café, sharing asparagus and artichoke as a piano played in the background. Many times we were approached by colleagues of Charles, and he would remark simple witty things and smile until they left. He refused to join each one at their table—punishing, perhaps, himself as well as me. By the time our dessert came, we were reserved perhaps, consigned to minuscule phrases and words:

"Delicious, isn't it?"

"Yes."

"This is your favorite, remember?"

That earned me a sour glance. "I'd forgotten," he said, slow and sonorous.

Eventually, I gave up. I left him to his sullen self once he'd pulled his wallet out and browsed the last of the open shops alone.

Nothing was of interest to me until I passed by an antique store I didn't recall ever entering before. Inside, it was immediately clear that the shop held a host of treasures, trinkets, and other miscellaneous items. There were toy soldiers, old records, and an inordinate amount of ancient McGuffey Readers. Thumbing through each one was like looking into a time machine—actually, the whole store seemed to have that effect, right down to the friendly old man at the counter.

I left feeling quite different than I had upon entering, but not due to the nostalgia of it all. In the glass case at the counter, I'd laid eyes on an item that I knew Charles would love. The porcelain woman was small, and her rosy-cheeked smile seemed contagious—I bought her immediately because she looked uncannily alike to his mother, the kindest woman I'd ever known. She had passed many years ago, but of course he'd never forgotten her. Like us, they'd always been close. Although . . . I guess everything has to end eventually. Charles had been so heartbroken when she died . . .

The man at the counter pulled me back into the present by placing the gift in my hands. The excitement of having it buoyed me as I went to find my husband again, pleasantly surprised when I noticed that he was just a few steps away. "Charles!" I called, but he didn't answer; he was enraptured—or perhaps enraged is a better word—with something on the other side of the street. His brows were knitted together, his mouth straightened into a menacing line. His nostrils flared like a bull's.

Feeling a chill in my body, I looked where he was looking—and it was Marjorie, staring back at him with the air of an uncertain animal, poised mid-stride with shopping bags in her hands. My breath caught, and I was reminded of that first moment when Charles had stepped over to me: *I know what you did.*

I looked back at him and then to Marjorie. We locked eyes. I was frightened by the intensity of her gaze, but trapped in the moment by forces beyond my control. I was helpless, pathetic, and impotent. No one moved.

Finally, I spoke. "Charles—"

He saw the paper-wrapped parcel in my hands and came to take it, though not with any positive emotion. He did it, I think, more out of obligation—or maybe out of some subconscious compassion, if any at all was left, that said it was wrong to trap his own sister beneath such an angry gaze, and to redirect it to his wife. This he did, and once it happened I watched Marjorie flee the scene for the second time in two days. He looked up too early after unwrapping the package—saw her running, swift as a doe—and it was then that the fury enveloped him completely.

It seemed almost unfair that what happened next came about so quickly. If a husband abandons his wife, shouldn't it take longer than the blink of an eye to occur? But it didn't matter, anyway. I got what was coming to me as Charles dropped what I had offered him, got in our car himself, and drove away, leaving me stranded amidst the sea of porcelain pieces: once a woman, now broken forever. Another attempt at peace—destroyed.

I came home hours later to a letter, tacked crookedly and carelessly to the door.

Marie,

I will never be able to forgive you. There's nothing else to it. You broke the most sacred bond between a man and woman: trust. Believe me when I say that there's nothing you can do to fix it.

I will come back eventually, but I need to be away from you right now. I don't know how long I'll be gone, but don't expect things to change when I get back. I will never love you again.

Charles

Instantly I was reminded of the paradox of the oranges: how they would grow so large and perfect that they'd cause their own demise, too heavy for the branches to hold.

In that moment, my heart was as heavy, and I fell to the ground like those citrus, watering the orange grove with my tears.

Walter Goes On A Date

C. W. Toledo

Long Beach, California - United States

Walter woke the same way he had for the past 83 years, slowly and then all at once. His eyes adjusted through the blurriness of the morning as he focused his vision on the fractured fractals and figments of faces of the plastered ceilings he had come to memorize over his decades of tracing the shapes as he fell asleep. He got out of bed the same way he had for the past 63 years: on the left side, tossing the soft cotton sheets off him, sending the pattern of dozens of sailboats in a tidal wave across the bed. It was a pattern he had hated, but the disputes over patterns and thread count now serve as a fond memory. He sat up quietly, as to not wake the other side of the bed, a practice in repetition and habit, even though the other side of the bed had been quiet for the last 10 years. Like memories, some habits never die.

Walter pulled himself out of bed, each year requiring more effort than the last. The weathering of the years weighed heavier and heavier on the muscles and joints that have moved him through this life. He stood to see himself in the mirror of his vanity only to face the visual interpretation of the work of the gravity of those years on the once taut face of his youth. Every day he remembered the words of his grandmother, "The more lines on your face, the fuller the life you've lived." While others ran from the signs of aging, Walter saw them as reminders of a life well-lived.

Walter sunk his toes into the softness of his house slippers, anchoring himself into the day to come. The once-proud stride of his youth was now replaced with a gentle shuffle across the hardwood floors of the house, he and his love had made a home. The sound of the slippers shuffling across the floor reverberated through the home, each step carried on the echoes of laughter and love that carried Walter through the best years of his life. Faces in pictures of moments long gone greeted him as he made his way to the kitchen. He couldn't help but smile back at the memories as they wished him a good day, even though he would be lying to himself if he ignored the reality that the joy of those memories was accompanied by an underlying sting. The photos now serve as a reminder that the partner who plotted and ployed their mutual euphoria had now been confined to the frames of the photos adorning the walls and the memories that grow hazier by the day. It's the sting that makes him stop at the end of the hall each morning to wish his love a good morning with a tender kiss. "Good morning, Clifford," he whispered as he placed his kiss on his hand, and his hand on the cheek of Clifford's portrait. It's been 10 years and that sting has never lessened or waned, rather Walter has learned to navigate around it. The pain of losing his better half wasn't temporary but terminal, a life sentence to be served through the memories that play on repeat in his mind.

However, today was different. Today the sting was masked by excitement. It was an excitement that Walter hadn't felt in years. Today there was prance in his step as he radiated because today Walter had a date. This was a date that Walter had been looking forward to, causing him to reckon with years of heartache, paired with uneasiness, but outweighed by the prospect of shaking his loneliness and emotional isolation. He reassured himself that everything would be okay as he traded his apprehension for an enthused anticipation. The high of it all delivered him to the kitchen, where his day would officially begin.

The little red light from the coffee pot shined up from the countertop across the kitchen, reminding him that he had never turned it off the day before. It was something that used to drive Clifford mad – "You know, you forgot to turn that thing off again," he would say. Walter used to hate being reminded of what he forgot, bothered that he could never seem to remember something so menial. Now it causes him to smile, convincing himself that it's just Clifford sending him a message from the beyond.

From the cabinet above his head, he pulled a box of his favorite cereal, foregoing the series of nutritional breakfasts that his daughter would insist are better for his health. Poor decisions can often times be sweeter than their alternatives, and this is always the case when it comes to breakfast cereal. He surmised that his overly-cautious daughter would never find out, the evidence of his dietary malfeasance would be hidden in the dishwasher before she arrived for her morning check-in. With cereal in a bowl and milk in hand, Walter brought himself to rest in the chair in the dining nook that he had called his own for decades.

In his mind, he could still see Clifford to his right, and their daughter, clamoring with excitement for the school day to come to his left. The soundtrack of lessons learned and playground gossip from eras ago play as Walter enjoyed his sugary breakfast delight. It warmed Walter that something as simple as sugar cereal could jog memories of moments passed. Even before the joy of their daughter shared breakfast with them at their nook, Clifford would pretend to be a mind reader, massaging Walters' scalp with his fingers as to receive intuitive vibrations informing him which breakfast item Walter would want. Most times, Clifford was right, leaving Walter wondering if he was truly psychic, or if their bond went so deep that he could accurately identify what he was craving through instinct.

His favorite breakfast cereals were always made sweeter with a side of warm memories.

"Dad, are you awake?" An anxious voice called out as the back door of the kitchen swung open. "Dad?" Walter began furiously shoveling heaps of sugared wheat bits into his mouth as his daughter entered the kitchen. "Dad! Why didn't you answer me?" She moaned as she set grocery bags on the kitchen island.

"I'm having breakfast," he replied through a mouthful of cereal.

"Dad, your grocery delivery was just sitting on the back porch, you can't leave them out there like that," she reprimanded as she put the perishable items away in the refrigerator. "Don't you read the notes I leave you on the breakfast table? They're to remind you to get your groceries." She grabbed a small stack of notes that she had left stuck on various bottles and surfaces that she would hope Walter would see. To her chagrin, Walter would collect these notes, stack them together, place them on the table, and forget them.

"I was hungry," Walter replied grouchily. He found it funny that roles tend to switch with age. It wasn't too long ago that he remembered chastising her for not cleaning her room or putting away her laundry, and now she's chastising him for not putting away his groceries.

"Is Matt here yet?" She asked with a sense of exasperation, peering at the cuckoo clock on the wall.

"Matt doesn't show up until 9 on Tuesdays," Walter replied.

"Dad, it's Friday, and that was your last caretaker, Rebecca, remember?" Her eyes dart to and from the clock as if it were a time bomb, ticking closer and closer to her explosion as she got closer and closer to being late to work. Her exasperation shifted to worry, as it often did when Walter appears confused as he was about Rebecca and Matt.

"Oh," Walter realized she was right. "You're right Taylor, you're always right," he replied, resigning to the idea that it would just be easier to acknowledge that she was probably right, rather than creating an argument over groceries, arrival times, or the litany of other concerns she probably has at this moment.

"What're you eating," she mumbled as she crossed the kitchen towards the dining nook. She kissed him on the head, before picking up the cereal box. A deep sigh exploded from her mouth. "Dad," she said with thick disappointment in her voice. "You can't eat cereal like this, your doctor warned you about this," almost as if she were scolding her children.

"That cereal tastes like cardboard," he exclaimed. "Besides, today's special, so I wanted to celebrate."

"What's going on today?" She replied with a profound sense of confusion. Did she forget an important date? Or was dad simply confused again?

"I have a date," he proclaimed with subtle confidence.

The kitchen grew silent as Taylor determined how to navigate this situation. "A date, huh?" She asked with a sense of put-on wonder.

"Yes, a date," Walter replied with collected confidence.

Taylor let out a small laugh. "With who, dad?"

"With a very respectable gentleman," Walter quipped with a sensible air in his voice, sensing her cynicism.

"Well, before your date tonight," Taylor mocked slightly, "remember that we're stopping by with the girls tonight"

"Shit," Taylor sighed, looking at her phone. "I'm gonna be late." She looked up to her father, as she began collecting her items. "Dad, please try to remember to take your medication, okay?"

Walter scoffed. He had long held the firm belief that any regiment of daily pills couldn't be good, and could simply be replaced with vitamins and hearty laughter. Although, so far he hadn't been able to find a doctor who subscribed completely to that same medicinal approach.

The back door flung open again, this time a well-dressed man in his 30s appeared in the kitchen. "I'm so sorry I'm late, the traffic on the 5 was horrible!" his words carried on gasps of breath as if he had just run a marathon.

"Matt, I mean, you can't be late like this," Taylor chided. "The groceries were on the back porch getting warm, dad was eating cereal that he knows isn't good for him," Walter sensed that that specific criticism was aimed at them both.

"I'm so sorry," Matt said, putting his hands up to ease the tension.

"Cut the boy some slack," Walter demanded from the table. "He's doing the best he can."

With a roll of her eyes, Taylor accepted her father's request, then leaned towards Matt. "I'm worried about him today," she said softly in an attempt to avoid her father's ears. "He's been a little confused today. He thinks he has a date tonight, so just . . . play along, okay? I'm going to call his doctor, I think it's getting worse," she said even softer, ladened with concern.

Matt nodded, acknowledging the severity of the situation Taylor just described. "I'll keep my eyes open for anything out of the ordinary. Delusions can be a warning sign that dementia is getting worse. I'll call you around noon."

"Thank you," she whispered. "Bye Dad," she called across the kitchen as she opened the back door. "Take it easy on Matt today, okay?"

With a mouthful of cereal, Walter raised his hand and waived, not taking his focus off of the delectable breakfast treat.

"Okay, Walter," Matt exclaimed with the typical vivacity he brought to the home each day. It was the demeanor that brightened the day of everyone who had the pleasure of coming into contact with him. "What's the plan for today?" he asked as he took a seat next to Walter. Taylor's old seat, in Walter's mind.

"Well," Walter leaned towards Matt, a cantankerous look in his eyes. "I've got a date tonight."

Matt bounced his shoulders in excitement as his face lit up. "Ooh, Walter, okay, okay! Tell me about him!"

Walter leaned back with a sense of secrecy, salivating in Matt's eagerness to learn more. "Well," he said with a sense of excitement, "he's quite the respectable gentleman."

"Does he treat you right?" Matt questioned with a feigned sense of defense. "He isn't going to hurt you, is he?"

Walter scoffed. "I wouldn't have any of that," he proclaimed loudly. "But we've got a busy day ahead of us, Matt. I need to get ready for tonight, and you're going to help me!"

"Okay," Matt agreed, leaning in towards Walter as they conspired the day's plans together. "What're we doing?"

"Well, I'm going to put on proper pants first," Walter laughed. "Then we need to go get my dry cleaning. I chose a special suit for today and had it cleaned last week."

"Wait a minute," Matt chimed up playfully, "You've had this date planned for at least a week and this is the first time you've told me?"

"I'm gentleman, Matt," Walter instructed with an air of self-assurance. "I keep romantic pursuits to myself."

Matt passed a small metal dish across the table and placed it in front of Walter. Walter peered in to see a collection of pills, pastilles, and lozenges aimed at promoting his health. A look of disgust contorted Walter's already wrinkled face.

"Walter," Matt warned the same way Walter used to when Taylor refused to eat her vegetables with dinner. And just like Taylor, Walter conceded and unhappily swallowed the collection of pills.

With a quick change of clothes, a spray of his favorite cologne, and brush through the few hairs remaining on his head, the two were out the door. In a daily ritual, Walter stopped to smell the roses in the garden between his front door and the rest of the yard.

"You know, Clifford and I planted these our first summer in this home," he told Matt as he bent over gently with a smile to smell the luscious red petals. "You might just see a bunch of roses, but they were something more to us. We wanted a home for so long," he laughed as he breathed in the gorgeous scent of the flowers. "These roses were a testament to the hard work that went into owning our own home." With a smile in his eyes, he quietly shared "and just like our own lives, some years they bloomed more beautifully than others, but they were still beautiful nonetheless." Walter gently plucked a rose from the bush. "They've never been this beautiful," he said softly as he tucked it into the boutonniere of his lapel. He stood in solemn reverence for a moment more as he appreciated the roses and all they've stood for and stood through over the years. With a smile on his face, he turned towards Matt and made his way to the car. "To the laundromat," Walter exclaimed as he lowered himself into Matt's sedan.

The drive along the tree-lined street hasn't changed much over the years, minus the ever-changing appearance of vehicles that adorn the driveways, and the occasional re-landscaping endeavors that shook up the sod, and with it certain members of the homeowners association. The neighbors have come and gone over the years, their children, just like Taylor, grew up and moved out. Some purchased the homes their parents owned and started their own family in the same fashion. The names changed with the families that came and went, but the love that filled the homes always remained the same.

The laundromat stood in the same place it had for years, despite the ever-changing city around it. Now tucked between two high-rise apartment buildings, the same family had been laundering Walter's clothes since he was a young man. In all that time, Walter never seemed to arrive when there wasn't a line. The photos of the family and their favorite clientele lined the wood-paneled walls of the laundromat. In an antiqued gold picture frame three frames to the left of the cash register, a younger Walter and Clifford stood displaying freshly laundered clothes in bags like fisherman displaying their daily catch.

"Walter, is that you?" Matt exclaimed with his usual sense of excitement, as they found their place in line. Walter couldn't determine if his excitement stemmed from just seeing him on the wall, or if it was because it was tucked between pictures of a famous actor and a First Lady. The location of their photograph on the wall was a point of pride for Walter and was occasionally used to fill the quiet space when the employee's behind the counter seemed less than eager to hold a conversation with him.

Walter nodded in response to Matt's question. "It's like you're almost famous!" he exclaimed, pointing at the other pictures on the wall. "The story behind it's even better," Walter laughed. He held the silence between them to build up the anticipation until Matt couldn't hold it any longer.

"You can't tell me you've got a good story and then not tell me," Matt explained.

"Well," Walter reminisced. "I remember that day so vividly. I mean, I don't know how I couldn't. We woke up, and I remember Clifford rolled over the way he used to. You know, he had the most brilliant blue-green eyes. They were the kind of eyes that would stop time, you know?"

"I've seen the pictures in the hallway, he did have beautiful eyes," Matt replied.

"Pictures never did his eyes justice. His eyes had a way of making me feel seen, unlike ever before." Walter stared and the picture of the younger him on the wall, wishing he could go back to that very moment.

"Walter," a friendly voice filled the air as the clerk behind the counter opened her arms. She always greeted him with the same level of enthusiasm, like two friends who had been parted for years.

"Agnes, you look as beautiful as ever!" Walter exclaimed as he crossed the lobby.

"Just one suit today?" she asked as she looked at the digital claim ticket on her computer. "Is that it?"

"That's it," Walter replied assuredly.

"Give me one sec, love," she motioned with a single index finger raised as she turned towards the rotating rows of people's prized pieces or wardrobe. Like clockwork, she stopped and pulled a single tweed suit from the dizzying array of textiles. With a smile Agnes turned around and handed the suit over to Walter, gently tucking the bottom of the plastic upwards to avoid it snagging on the counter. "Have a good day, Walter."

"How much is it," Walter asked, only to be met with Agnes' arms waving across her body.

"Not today, Walter," she replied. "It's on us,"

"Bah!" he exclaimed. "Let me pay."

"Walter," she replied sternly, peering at him from behind the thick plastic frames of her eyeglasses.

Walter knocked his wallet on the counter before tucking it away into his suit jacket pocket. "You know," he said slyly. "I've got a date tonight."

"Is that what the suit's for?" Agnes asked playfully.

Walter nodded proudly as a warm smile melted across Agnes' face. "What a lucky man they are, you're going to look as handsome as ever!" she said warmly. She looked softly towards Matt, and Matt nodded back. This was the unspoken language between onlookers on Walter's "bad days." A mix of concern dotted with sympathy but supported by a deep sense of care for the carefree gentleman.

"So long, Agnes," Walter called out as he crossed the threshold of the laundromat, waving his arm above his head. It was Walter's trademark farewell.

A gentle mid-morning breeze blew down the street. Over the years parking had grown more difficult on this street, so the two had to make a small trek to return to space where they parked. "So, you didn't finish your story!" Matt reminded him.

"Oh, yes!" Walter exclaimed, trudging slowly the breeze blowing at his face. "Well, Clifford stared at me with those eyes. Then he asked me if I wanted to go on an incredible adventure with him."

"What was the adventure?" Matt pressed.

Walter laughed. "He didn't tell me right away. He walked me to the closet, and he just started picking out our suits. I wanted to ask him what we were doing, but he kept digging and I dug right there with him. We picked out 4 suits each. They weren't expensive or flashy, but they were the best we had."

The car beeped as they grew closer. Matt opened the back door and hung the clothes from a hook above the seat. "Hold on, I want to hear the rest of this, but where to now, Walter?" Matt asked, closing the back door. "Are we going home?"

"Nope!" he replied shortly.

"Where to now?"

Walter threw his arm up behind his head and pointed to the sign on the building behind them.

"The barbershop?" Matt asked.

"Yup!"

"Did you make a reservation?"

"Yup!" Walter quipped again. "I told you this morning, that's why I thought you parked here!"

Matt smiled as he replayed the morning back in his entirety. Realizing that Walter never mentioned a reservation, he began to believe that today wasn't a great day for Walter. He smiled and nodded. "Let's check it out," he said as he locked the car, a honk alerting them both the deed had been done.

As they entered the barbershop, Walter pointed up at the red, white, and blue barbers' pole that slowly turned as they approached the door. "You know, my grandfather was a barber," Walter shared with Matt. "He would tell me 'Walter, only go to barbers with this pole. That means they're unionized.'"

Walter turned and looked at Matt sternly. "Are you in the union?"

"I don't think I have a union," Matt replied with uncertainty.

Walter shook his head vigorously. "Unacceptable," he snapped. "Everyone should have a union."

The inside of the shop was small and smelled heavily of hair products.

"Hey, hey, Walter," the stocky barber called out across the shop, approaching with his hands outstretched for a handshake. "How're you doin, my man?"

Walter grasped his hand firmly. "I'm well, Joe, I'm well, how're you?"

"Good, good," he replied. "My chair's right over here," he motioned, gently leading Walter across the room to the overstuffed barber chair on the other side of the shop. The space had a classy, vintage feel. Black and gold calligraphy adorns the space, harkening the barbershop heyday of the 1900s. With such an elevated ambiance, it's no surprise Walter called this his shop.

"So what're we doing today, Walt?" Joe said, tossing the apron over Walter, tossing his hair through his fingers.

"I was thinking I might go for a bouffant today, really shake things up a bit," his teeth, crooked with age, reflected his humor through the mirror before him. Joe burst out into a laugh, reaching for his scissors from the counter in front of them.

"Bouffant, huh? I was thinking you could really work the French braid!"

The irony of these suggestions for Walters' lack of hair always brightened the mood of the already vivacious barbershop. Joe grabbed his shears from the countertop, paired them with a comb, and began to work through Walter's fine hair.

"Whatever you do, make it nice." Walter warned. "I have a date tonight, and I need to look my best."

"A date, huh?" Joe replied, gently snipping away at the various dead ends and fly-aways across Walter's head. "Well, we're gonna make sure you're in the best shape possible."

A television in the corner quietly aired a game to the small barbershop. It was enough to pull Walter in. Televisions have always served as kryptonite to Walter, no matter what happens to be on the screen, he's bound to watch. Over years of falling into this inevitable trap, he has learned to compensate for his flaw by asking others in the room something about what's on television, thus centering everyone's attention on the TV.

"How's this season looking for LA?" He asked Joe, breaking his laser focus from his hair.

"How's any season looking for LA," he bemoaned, dredged with cynicism. "They're doing okay, but you know how it goes."

Walter laughed and shook his head. He had absolutely no idea what Joe meant, but he pretended. He really didn't care what the sport was, he was a Los Angeles fan through and through. If LA had an underwater basket-weaving team, Walter would be their number one fan.

"You know, I could never watch sports with Clifford," Walter said to the two men in the barbershop.

"Why's that," Joe asked, snipping away at Walter's hair.

"Oh, boy!" Walter exclaimed. "I tried to get him over to the stadium a few times to watch a baseball game. He would always ask: 'What's the point? What happens when our teams win? Do our charities get money? Do the professional leagues build better schools in our community?'" Walter laughed at himself. "I never had an answer for him. I would tell him that we would have a sense of pride in ourselves, and you know what he'd say?"

"What's that?" Matt asked eagerly, a smile on his face, his jacket tucked in his arms as he took in every word of Walter's story.

"He would say: 'I already live in the greatest city in the world, I don't need a trophy to tell me what I already know.'"

"That's why I always liked him more," Joe teased as he gently teased Walters' wispy hair with a comb.

"You and me both," Walter said, his laughter carried a different timbre as he tried to hide just how much he missed Clifford. Over the last 10 years, he learned how to mask his pain with a smile, divert his pain with a laugh, but over the last 10 years, the pain of missing his better half never subsided, but rather grew more fierce with each passing day.

"You all don't understand, it took us years to move here!" Walter shifted the conversation to distract him from his hurt. "We had dreamed of living here from when we first met. We planned and we conspired, and every time we'd jump, the winds would take us somewhere else. Albuquerque, Reno, Ann Arbor, all the while, we wanted to be here."

"So what brought you here?" Joe asked.

"Well, when you love something that much, you say 'to hell with it,' and you do whatever you can to end up with him."

The Freudian slip wasn't missed by either of the men in the shop, but it wasn't new to them either. In their ways, with their own experiences with Walter, they both knew how much he missed Clifford.

"That's how we met Joe," Walter said, slightly turning between razor adjustments to look at Matt. "He was the first barber we had here!"

"I still remember that first cut," Joe chimed in.

"You do, huh?"

"Of course I do," Joe said. "You were one of my first appointments out of barber school, and you were 45 minutes late. You threw off my whole day, I almost got fired," Joe laughed.

"Too bad," Walter joked. "I would've saved myself the embarrassment of years of your haircuts."

"Yeah, but that wouldn't have done anything about your face," Joe clapped back in his usual banter. The two men laughed as Joe removed the chair cloth from Walter, holding a mirror up to show Walter the back of his head. Walter didn't care. These haircuts were less aesthetic, and more about the visit.

"Looks as bad as always," Walter laughed.

"Do you think your date tonight is going to like it?" Joe asked, acknowledging how excited Walter was when he walked into the shop.

"I have a feeling he's going to love it!" Walter replied, admiring himself in the mirror.

Joe helped Walter out of his seat, and over to Matt. The three men walked over to the cash register and settled the cost of the trim. With a series of witty jabs and laughs, Walter and Matt left the shop and entered the car.

"Where to now?" Matt asked, turning on the car.

"I'm a little hungry, how 'bout we grab some lunch?" Walter offered. "My treat."

"Sure, where sounds good to you?"

"There's a little sandwich shop by the park by my house. Let's go there and eat in the park, sound good?"

It didn't take long to show up at the sandwich shop, where Walter ordered a salad and sparkling water. The two men walked behind the shop and found a bench in the middle of the park, shaded by a few birch trees. They unpacked their lunches and began to enjoy eating.

"You not hungry today, Walter?" Matt asked as he unwrapped his rather large sandwich, looking on to Walter's measly salad.

"I told you, I have a date tonight, I don't want to stuff myself today," Walter replied matter-of-factly.

"Tell me more about that, where did you two meet?"

"We met at a musical production," Walter said, placing a forkful of coniferous greens into his mouth.

"Was it that play that Taylor took you to a few weeks back?" Matt's question was met with a few shakes of Walter's head.

"Our eyes met after the show, and there was something so familiar," Walter smiled. "He finally decided that tonight was the night."

"That's cute," Matt said between bites.

Walter smiled as he continued to take bites of his salad. It was an excitement he hadn't felt in years: the excitement of something new, paired with the feeling of being wanted. At the same time, he had to reconcile these feelings with the feelings of sadness, knowing he could be leaving behind what he and Clifford had built.

"You never finished your story from earlier," Matt reminded Walter.

"What story?"

"The story of the photograph on the wall of the laundromat."

"Oh!" Walter exclaimed, "Where'd I leave off?"

"The suits!"

"Oh yes!" He laughed. "We wanted to match, but we were so young, and didn't have the money for new suits. So we had everything we could possibly have that matched dry-cleaned. Agnes's shop was the only shop that could do it as quickly as we needed it done! Of course, at the time it was her mom's shop." Walter took a deep sip of the sparkling water, and let the breezy sunlight hit his face. It was warm, but the memory made him feel so much warmer.

"He explained to her what he had planned for the day and needed them as quickly as possible. She waived the express fees and gave us a discount. She snapped that picture of us as we were headed to the courthouse!"

"And they've left that photo up ever since?" Matt asked.

"Ever since. She said we were one of those couples where you could just feel the love between the two of us. She said it reminded her that true love was real and it was out there, so she kept that photo up."

"No way!" Matt exclaimed through a rather large bite of his vegan turkey sandwich.

"True love is usually just waiting right under our noses, waiting for those moments when we're not looking to pop up and sweep us off our feet."

Matt gently raised his eyebrows while discreetly rolling his eyes.

"Do you not believe me?" Walter replied.

"I just don't think it's out there for me," Matt admitted.

"What? Love?" Walter snapped back.

"Yeah, I just..." Matt wiped his face with a napkin. "I've just become accustomed to the idea that I'll spend the rest of my life alone."

"Why's that?"

"It's not that important," Matt tried to deflect.

"Matt, when it comes to love, there are few things more important," Walter reminded him.

"It's hard, you know?" Matt admitted. "I'm not the skinniest man out there, and I'm not the most attractive man in the world, I'm just not anyone's type."

"So why are you wasting your time chasing people who aren't worth your love?" Walter asked.

"That's a good question," Matt rolled up his sandwich wrapper.

"You have a big heart, and anyone in this city would be lucky to call you their better half. The right one is going to see that."

"Thanks, Walter," Matt replied, taking Walter's words with a grain of salt. He dismissed it as those words that people who are happily married say to their single friends to make them feel less disenchanted. "So what about this date tonight?"

"I'm excited about it," Walter said with a soft smile. "But it's just a date. Who knows what'll happen."

"I guess that's a good way of looking at it," Matt replied. "What time is he picking you up?"

"He said 8 pm, but we're both old so who knows if he'll remember," Walter laughed.

"Do you think he's going to forget?" Matt asked, getting up from the table.

"I don't know," Walter said, joining him by standing up. "But either which way, I'm going to be prepared for him."

"I don't think he'll forget about you," Matt consoled him.

"I sure hope so," Walter replied, brushing the dust from the bench off his pants and joining Matt on the pavement. Off in the distance, children swung from a play set, screams of delight filled the air. For a moment, Walter was a young father, watching Taylor effortlessly swing from the bars, and bolt down the slide. It was the days of impossibly big dreams that left little room for fear. Where she was invincible and impervious to everything, but a simple kiss could fix all of life's boo-boos. A good day was measured in laughter and ice cream, and dinner times were bartered with "five more minutes." They were the strongest super-heroes paled in comparison to daddy, who could fix everything from imaginary castles to hurt feelings. Those days slipped away faster than Walter would've liked, leaving him wondering whether or not he took them for granted. He would give anything to go back to those days, but those days only live in his mind and gilded frames along his hallways.

"You okay, Walter?" Matt asked, rubbing his back gently.

"Yeah," Walter smiled, turning to face him. "Taylor used to play on that play set when she was a little girl," the beauty of those moments rested in a smile on his face. "Would you mind running one more errand with me?"

"Anything," Matt replied.

A short car ride across the interstate, and the two had swapped the spruces of the lively park for the clamor of a packed market space. Vendor stalls lined the narrow passageways. Smells from foods, familiar and exotic, filled the space with a mouth-watering aroma. Walter wobbled his way through the crowd, clumsily weaving through the spaces between shoppers. Matt followed closely. The two made their way through the crowded center of the marketplace, and off to the fringe corners, where fewer shoppers populated the corridors. Handmade tchotchkes and crafts of every color and size hung from the stalls, begging to be purchased by the passersby. As alluring as some of them may have been, they weren't alluring enough to dissuade Walter from his mission.

A small stall tucked near the corner of the marketplace is where Walter finally came to a stop. With small vials and bottles filled with amber liquid, he knew he had finally found the place. He turned to Matt with a look of certainty on his face, his eyebrows raised in excitement with the secret he was about to bestow upon Matt.

"I've traveled to some of the most incredible places on Earth, and have shopped in some of the finest designer stores on the globe, but there is no better perfumery on the planet than this one right here."

"Really," Matt replied, impressed with the glowing review this small, out-of-the-way booth just received.

"Is Millie here today?" Walter asked the young woman standing at the counter.

"No, she's been at our main store in the Bay Area this week," she smiled, "Do you need me to give her a message?"

Walter scrunched his face and swatted his hand. "Bah, no," his face rearranged itself to a smile. "I wouldn't bother you with all of that, just wanted to say hi is all." Walter turned towards Matt. "You know, Millie is the owner of this store. She made all these colognes and perfumes you see here!" Without waiting for Matt's response, he turned back towards the clerk. "How are you today?"

"Oh, I'm well, thanks! How are you? Can I help you find anything?" She responded, eager to help Walter find the right scent.

"I'm well, thank you for asking!" Walter replied sweetly. "Do you have any bottles of Desert Rose?"

"Indeed we do, right here!" She leaned over the long rows of perfume and handed Walter a bottle with a gold and black label on it. Desert Rose.

Walter gently took the bottle from her hand, took off the gold lid, and took a deep breath in while smelling the nozzle of the cologne. With his eyes closed, a large smile overtook his face as he was transported somewhere more peaceful than the overcrowded marketplace. Wherever he went, he stayed there for a few moments before returning and opening his eyes.

"I'll take it," he said, reaching into his coat pocket to hand her his credit card.

"Desert Rose," Matt said with a sense of disbelief, inspecting the bottle closely. "I never would've taken you as a floral scent kind of guy."

Walter laughed as the clerk handed him the credit card back to him with his receipt. "Yeah, I wasn't at first. I almost hated it." He put the credit card in his pocket. "But it's funny how things grow on you."

Walter turned to Matt and gave him a nod, and started to walk away from the stand before feeling his pant pockets, the expression on his face tightening.

"Did you lose something?" Matt asked.

Walter let out a confused sigh. "I don't think she gave me my change," Walter mumbled before quickly turning to the perfume stand to confront the sales person. Matt bounded after Walter.

"Sir, you paid with a credit card," she informed Walter, who stood at the counter adamant that he paid with cash, and frustrated that she would lie about it.

"I gave you $60, I know I did."

"No Sir, you paid with a credit card, I can show you the receipt if you'd like," she offered politely but firmly.

Walter grew irate as he opened his wallet. "I had sixty dollars right here this morning. I know I did. My husband gave it to me before I left this morning."

Matt gently grabbed Walter's arms, and tried to sooth the angry gentleman. "Walter," he said softly, "Hey Walter, why don't you look at me."

"No," Walter yelled, drawing the attention of the shoppers around him. "She stole my money. I want my money back." He reached in his coat pocket to pull out his phone. "I'm going to call my husband," he threatened the woman. "He won't be happy."

He pulled out his phone, but couldn't get it to unlock, making him angrier.

"Walter, I have an idea," Matt offered in a calm voice. "Why don't I come back later with a receipt to get your money, okay?"

"You'll get my money?" The shift in Walter's tone signaled that this could be a viable option.

"Yeah," Matt replied with a smile. "I'll come back, and speak to the manager, and get your money."

"Okay," Walter replied with hesitation. "But I'm still calling Clifford."

Matt put his hand on the phone and gently pushed it down. "Why don't we call him from the car, okay?"

"Who are we calling from the car?" Walter asked.

"I said why don't we get to the car, okay?" Matt replied.

"Yeah, that sounds nice," Walter responded with a smile. He nodded to the confused woman sitting behind the counter, as he turned and shuffled towards the exit. Matt took a sigh of relief. Episodes such as that were becoming more and more frequent, even though they last all of a few seconds. He knew he would have to keep a closer eye on Walter.

Walter passed through the market, past the stalls filled with vibrant colors and loud voices. The rich smell of the diverse flavors of the market ceased at the main entrance as the two passed a flower cart, emitting the most beautiful floral scent the two had ever smelled. It was enough to remind Walter of one more thing he had to do before his date.

"Oh! I have one more thing I have to do today," Walter said, suddenly remembering what he had set out to do that morning.

"Sure, what is it," Matt asked.

"First, I need your help picking out some flowers," Walter turned and began smelling the flowers of the stand.

"What kind are you looking for?" Matt asked while joining Walter in smelling the flowers.

"Well, I know he likes roses," he said softly, nose deep in an array of lilies. "And sunflowers," he added as he made his way across the row of flowers. "And peonies," he remembered, as he began to admire the wall of flowers behind him. "And ranunculuses," he concluded as he selected a white bouquet, complete with white roses, peonies, ranunculuses, cut with brilliant bursts of yellow sunflowers.

"Perfect," he exclaimed after a brief inspection of the flowers. "He's going to love them!"

The two traded the bustle of the city faded to serenity beyond the wrought iron gates. The grass was perfectly trimmed along the tree-lined streets which Walter used to struggle to navigate through. "Left, left, past the fountain, pull to the right." The directions have eventually succumbed to ritual, this particular path was taken nearly every day.

Matt pulled the car over to the curb and put it in park. He turned off the car, and let his hands fall to his lap while Walter took a deep breath. His chest held the airtight the way heavy hearts hopelessly grasp for moments before they turn into memories, only to tarnish and fade with time.

Walter grabbed the flowers, opened the car door, and slowly made his way over the perfectly manicured grass, leaving Matt and the car behind him. Every detail etched into his memory from the first time he ever visited this place. 57 steps from the curb, careful the sprinkler head that doesn't retract all the way, and the small divot in the grass just deep enough to catch an unsuspecting heel. Focus on the steps, cognizant of the breaths, or you'll lose yourself in the pain.

The bronze nameplate shone in the dazzling mid-afternoon sun, laid on the grass like an autumn leaf, that surreal reminder that dog days of summer have come and gone, while the uncertainty and the chill of the fall sets in. Walter bent over and placed the fresh flowers into the vase next to the nameplate that shared his last name. The hurt held heavy in Walter's chest, a pain that others said would eventually fade, a false statement that only eventually added anger to his heartache.

"I saw these today and immediately thought of that time we ate at that restaurant that had fresh flowers that hung from the ceiling. I just had to get them." Walter spoke softly to the grave, almost as if he expected Clifford to speak back, and somewhere in Walter's subconscious, he is.

"We waited for hours to get that table, even though we had a reservation, remember?" a smile cracked across Walter's face. "And since I was so infatuated with the flowers above us and the flowers on the table, you felt justified in grabbing the bouquet from the table, hiding it under your coat, and surprising me with it as we left." A gentle laugh left Walter's smile. "When the host realized what you had done, he chased after us, and we ran blocks and blocks, and blocks, laughing and laughing!" Walter sat in the warmth of the memory, because for just a split-second, Clifford was right there with him, running down 6th street with a bouquet in one hand and my heart in the other.

The warmth faded, and reality sunk back in. Walter stood in the empty graveyard, looking down upon the final resting place of his better half. Sometimes he couldn't help getting angry at Clifford as he stood there. They promised every adventure with each other, never letting each other face the unknown without them. Now Walter stood here, having illicit affairs with the memories with the man he spent his life with, only to watch them die over and over again.

"I have to tell you something, and I don't want you to get disappointed with me," he wrung his hands together nervously. "I'm getting prepared for that date tonight. I have Matt taking me around collecting things, getting me ready." Tears began to fill his eyes, as he looked up to the sky for clarity. He hung his head back down to finish his confession. "The best part of my day was always when you came through the door at the end of the day. Every day. And for the last 10 years, I've waited. I've held my breath, and I've pleaded to the universe that I was lost in a nightmare. But you never did." Walter caught his breath, as the tightness in his chest clenched his heart.

"I've tried. You know that? I tried so hard, trying to pick up the pieces since you left, but I can't. I thought it would get easier, but every day I wake up next to the space you've laid for decades, and I make the same breakfast I've made every day since we met, and I wait. I wait for you to come down from our room. I wait for you to sit at the table. I wait for you to take my hand. I wait, and I wait, and I wait, and you never come." He condemns his dearly departed as tears stream down his face. "I never imagined a world so lonely, so empty, so . . . hollow."

He bent down on his knees, something his doctors had warned him a million times to avoid, and he laid a kiss on the nameplate that sparkled in the daylight. "I hope you're not disappointed, and I hope you can grow to forgive me. My love for you hasn't faded in the slightest, even after that day you came to rest here. Always remember that."

A sob cut through his sentence, cutting the words short, but letting the pain hang in the air, the way it did on that overcast Sunday when his body was buried in this spot.

"Always." He reminded him as he stood up, pulling his handkerchief from his pocket to wipe his tears.

"Walter?" Matt called, as he approached him in this sacred place. "I know I don't usually do this, but you know you're not supposed to use your knees like that. Do you need help getting back up?"

"Thank you, Matt," Walter nodded, holding his arm out for support getting off the ground, all while avoiding his teary eye contact with Matt.

Matt helped Walter off the ground, then stood awkwardly for a moment, debating whether or not to comfort or to head back to the car. How does one comfort someone who has lost half their world?

"He would've really liked you, Matt," Walter admitted, warming the space between him and Matt.

"He sounds like a great man," Matt said, as he slowly walked closer, taking in the name and the dates on the gravestone.

"Great could never describe him well enough," Walter whispered, adding weight to Matt's comments.

"You never finished your story you were telling me earlier," Matt reminded him.

"What story?"

"The one you started telling me at the laundromat?"

"What laundromat?" Walter replied, confused at Matt's comments.

Matt relied on his training to navigate the situation. "Oh, you were just telling me a story that you didn't finish is all…"

"Ah," Walter nodded his head slightly, and then returned his eyes down to the grave. "You know, growing up I read the greatest stories of love and adventure, each of them tucked away gently with the happiest of ever afters. I've watched those stories become movies, celebrated and revered. I've watched people strive to have lives like those on the pages."

Walter sighed.

"We were one of those stories. In fact, we were the greatest love story ever told. We were the kind of story that would just leave you wondering how could the story get any better than this? And then inevitably, it would, again and again." He clenched the handkerchief in his hands the way the loneliness clenched his chest. "We never got our own novel. Our love wasn't celebrated by the masses. We were the only ones to ever know it, and that made it all the more special. We never got the ending we imagined we would. We never got the ending we deserved. Instead, I'm here, holding all these memories alone, trying not to let them slip away. Yet every day, more and more of our story fades into history."

He looked up at Matt, the tears heavy in his eyes.

"Sometimes, the story never gets an ending. That's the unfortunate side of life. And we'll spend the rest of our time trying to craft the perfect sentence that would wrap the story up in the happiest way. We'll artfully craft hypotheticals and brilliant what-ifs, but it never changes the fact that the story ended where it did, and we'll never get that ending we dreamed of."

Walter turned and patted his hand on Matt's shoulder, as he stood there dumbfounded. Walter tried to cover his pain with a smirk, as he started back towards the car.

He paused for a moment, turned towards Clifford's resting place again. "The kids'll be alright," he said with a gentle sniffle as he turned and made his way to the car. Cognizant of the breaths, focusing on his steps, careful of the divot that would catch the unsuspecting heel, and the sprinkler head that doesn't retract all the way. He finished his 57th step, and opened up the door of the car, taking his seat in the sun-warmed sedan. He was ready.

The drive home was quiet. Walter reclined in the passenger side seat and let himself bask in the sunlight that flooded through the sunroof of Matt's sedan. The rumble of the road on the tires gently rocked him to sleep. Walter's mood swings weren't new to Matt, and in fact, they've grown increasingly more and more common as his dementia began to worsen. He's begun to take a mental inventory of episodes, ready to report to Taylor when she calls at the end of the day. Until then, Matt was prepared to spend the rest of the day in silence as Walter continued to nap.

The old driveway often thrashed the car from side to side as it pulled in from the road. Sometimes being enough to wake Walter from his sleep. On the day's it wouldn't, Matt would let the car run, and sit in silence until Walter woke up. Today appeared to be one of those days.

Walter laid in the passenger seat, his mouth agape as he rested peacefully in the sun. Matt put the car in park, and let the car idle. He pulled his phone from his pocket and opened up his messages. He had one unread message notification, the same notification he's had since 7:36 am, but he never had the gumption to read it. His finger hovered over the message, the name Felice in bold at the top of his messages.

Matt took a deep breath, and looked over to Walter, deep in his slumber. Most days, Matt sits and listens to Walter, and imagines himself and Felice as the main characters in similar stories, with a love just as deep and a connection as rare. He was inspired by their love and was sometimes secretly jealous of it. It was one of those loves that seemed to freeze time, enrapturing all those who had the privilege of standing in its presence. It was so fervid that it would transcend time and space, and though Matt had never met Clifford, he could feel him standing in the room as Walter lost himself in the memories of their better days. Most days, it was the doubt that he could ever find love as powerful as the one Walter and Clifford shared that kept Matt from replying to unopened messages. After today, it was the fear of losing that love before he was ready to let go.

Walter gently shook his head from side to side as he woke, trying to make sense of his surroundings. "Perfect timing," Matt exclaimed as he turned off the car. "We just pulled up!"

Walter laughed out loud. "What can I say, I've always had a good sense of time!" He unbuckled himself and got out of the car. Matt looked back down on the phone on his lap. A message named Felice begging to be responded to. Disappointment with himself caused his brow to furrow as he put the phone back into the pocket of his coat, leaving the message unread, an endeavor to tackle his insecurities at a later time.

As they entered the home through the front door, the smell of sage and piñon flooded the air, and with it a million little memories, spilling like glitter. Some memories are happier than others, but each one served as a reminder of the long life he was so lucky to have lived. To Walter, that meant home. He held the frame of the door, and lifted his feet one by one over the threshold, remembering the days when it was easier to walk into this home. The discomfort in his knees as they bent upward was aided by the memory of him and Clifford crossing that threshold for the first time, having a place to call home. The million seemingly insignificant times this door opened, to greet, to part, to welcome, and to share the warmth of the home they had built together. The million little moments Taylor would enter and leave through these doors, from first days of school to last days of living at home. From kindergarten recitals to prom, to graduation. From the first time he met his grandchildren, to the last time he crossed the threshold with an ailing Clifford, this simple entryway has captured almost all of his life's moments.

"You okay?" Matt asked as he outstretched his hands to help Walter through the door.

Walter smiled politely back up at Matt as he lifted his left foot to meet the rest of his body inside the home. The two made their way to the kitchen, where Walter took his usual seat at the kitchen table, which lay somewhere under pill bottles, newspapers, and bills. If Clifford could see this mess, he would lose his mind. Matt rattled briefly through the kitchen and returned with a full glass of water for Walter, and opened a series of pill bottles to dispense the proper cocktail of taupe and white pills of various sizes aimed at keeping the human pieces of Walter firmly planted on this earth. He took them begrudgingly with a large gulp of water.

"It was the day we got married," Walter let out with a breath, folding his hands in his lap. Matt's brow furrowed, unsure of what he was talking about. "The story that I forgot I was telling earlier," Walter reminded him, "It was the day we got married."

A smile broke across his face as he recalled the memory. "We had it all planned. We had sent out invitations, we had sent out save-the-dates, we had done the whole thing. I remember that I was in the middle of pulling up various caterers and vendors when he stopped me in my tracks and said 'let's just get married.'"

Matt loved the look in Walter's eyes when he recollects memories, and this moment was no exception. It's almost as if he's back in that moment himself, standing there with Clifford, once again laying the foundation of their lifelong love.

"We got every suit we had dry-cleaned, we made an appointment with the justice of the peace, and we went down to the court the next day and got married. That picture in the dry-cleaners was their way of celebrating with us."

"That's so sweet," Matt replied with a smile on his face. "You two were a beautiful couple."

Walter peered up at Matt from his water cup, giving him a gentle huff. The two sat in silence for a moment.

"So tell me more about your date," Matt pried.

"What time is it now?" Walter asked, turning to look at the clock on the wall, knowing full well he wouldn't be able to see the hands on the clock.

"Four-thirty-five," Matt replied.

"Ah, well he'll be here later tonight," Walter confirmed, with a nod.

"Where did you two meet again?" Matt asked, aiming to create small talk until 5 pm when Taylor usually comes to check in on Walter.

"You know, you ask me a lot of questions about my dates, but I don't know too much about who you're dating or what's new in your life" Walter quickly quipped.

Matt smirked and sat in silence for a moment, taken aback by the sentiment. It dawned on him that he had spent the last few years asking Walter about the smallest details of his life, but hasn't shared much of his own story with Walter.

"I've seen the look on your face when you look at your phone, Matt. Anyone who has been in love knows that look all too well."

Matt laughed sheepishly. "What look," he asked in hopes of throwing Walter off the scent.

"Oh, Matt," Walter began to laugh. "I've worn that look before, not for a while now, but I've worn it."

Matt, knowing he had been caught, hung his head and let out a nervous laugh to himself, letting silence rest in between the pill bottles and old newspapers on the kitchen table.

"Our hearts tell us to let go of our inhibitions and our insecurities, and to fall fully into the arms of those who we think could be the one, but our heads have us convinced that we're not worthy of being loved. That no matter how hard we've worked to polish our deepest scars, our flaws aren't worth being loved," Walter let his knowledge lift the silence that filled the room.

Shyly, Matt raised his head to meet Walter's eyes. "Did you feel that way with Clifford?"

"Did I feel that way when the most perfect man in the world gave me his phone number and asked me to dinner?" Walter asked sarcastically. "Did I let every scrap of insecurity build up the biggest wall around my heart? You bet I did. I couldn't convince myself that I was worth loving the way I knew he wanted to love me."

"So what did you do?" Matt asked.

"I fell," Walter replied. "I fell. Despite the fears and insecurities that told me I couldn't be loved, I took the chance. And you know what? I never looked back."

Walter reached across the table and held Matt's hand in his. "And as I sit here wishing I could have one more minute with him, for one more dance in front of the fireplace, to hear his laugh fill this space, I realize that every moment I spent trying to convince myself that I wasn't good enough for his love was another moment we could've had together." Walter shook Matt's hand, causing him to lift his head again. "Life is short, I'm telling you that now. If you even think that this one might be the one, go for it. Go all in. Fall, unencumbered. Be a fool in love."

"What if she isn't?" Matt replied.

"Well, I suppose you would know better than I," Walter replied. "And I suppose you could go through this life, guarding your heart and living tightly behind the walls you've convinced yourself you've needed. But I'll say this, I would go through every ounce of heartache and pain I had experienced all over again if I knew Clifford was waiting for me at the end of it all."

The conversation hung in the air between them until it eventually succumbed to the gentle hum of the refrigerator behind them. Walter leaned himself back in his chair and took in a deep breath, uncertain of how his conversation landed with Matt.

"Truth be told, our first hello led to a first date. That first date led to a first kiss. That first kiss led to us saying 'I do.' Those 'I do's,' led to our first home and our first child. If I would've believed all the reasons I wasn't worthy of being loved, I would've missed all the things in my life that I truly love."

Matt nodded his head softly and gave a smirk while rolling his lips against his teeth. The conversation ended there, though Walter had hoped that his message had landed upon the young man.

"And thank you," Walter added.

"For what?" Matt replied.

"I get confused sometimes," Walter admitted. "I hate that. I hate that part of me. But you never make it this big deal. You still see me as a human, and not everyone does. So thank you."

"Of course," Matt extended his hand to hold Walter's. "That's why I'm here."

"Hello," the disembodied voice of Taylor filled the kitchen from the back door, cutting through the conversation like a rapier. Matt curled his lips, acknowledging to Walter that somewhere and somehow, his words landed. Taylor traipsed across the kitchen with bags in her hand, placing them on the island before heading over to kiss Walter on the head.

"What'd you do today?" Taylor asked while patting Matt on the back, standing behind the two men sitting at the table.

Walter smiled and leaned back in his chair to get a better look at his daughter. "We got ready for my date tonight," Walter replied happily.

"Oh yeah?" Taylor replied with cynicism wrapped in padded gloves. "Well, I hope you don't plan on going to dinner, the girls wanted to stop by before robotics tonight so I brought dinner from Orlando's. Sound good?"

Walter stood up slowly, peeling himself from the dining room chair. It was the time of day where Taylor expected to talk to Matt about how he did during the day, talking as if he wasn't in the room, even if he was at the same table. Over time, he's come to realize that it's more comfortable to retreat to another room than it is to watch two people discuss the minutiae of his life as if he's just a passenger.

"It sounds great, I'll just get a salad on my date," he winked to Taylor as he removed himself from the dining room.

"Has this dating thing been going on all day?" Taylor asked Matt as Walter left the room. "I worry about him, he hasn't really talked to anyone outside this home in the last few months, and now he thinks he has a . . ." The conversation faded into floral patterned wallpaper of the plush sitting room where Walter decided to resign. The room had remained relatively unedited over the last few decades, with the exception of a series of trinkets and baubles that the granddaughters had gifted Walter over the last few years. The resoluteness of the room served as a trigger for Taylor, who constantly suggests some change or renovation that needs to be made whenever she enters the room. Bay windows would bring in more light, wallpaper could make this space more modern, or these chairs have seen better days. All of which were undoubtedly true, Walter would admit to himself. But this room is more than that, as is the rest of the home. It's not about the livability of the space, but the life that occurred in that space. This sitting room is the one room that hasn't become overrun with pill bottles, prescription notes, doctors' instructions, gels, creams, salves, heating pads, handles, bars, remotes, or the litany of other artifacts reserved for the aged. Rather, it serves as a memorial of the life that was lived in this home. In this room, Clifford is alive.

He's alive in the photographs that adorn the marbled bookshelves on either side of the fireplace. He's alive in the matching quatrefoil patterned armchairs they picked out when they bought the home and placed them within arm's reach so they could reach each other. He's alive in the spot where the Christmas tree would be placed every year, where he would meticulously place each wrapped gift for that perfect holiday-card feeling. He's alive in the dust that catches the beams of sun that break through the sheer curtains drawn over the windows. His life touched every piece of this room, and his life continues to live on in every piece of this room. In the years following his death, Walter avoided this room like he avoided the reality that Clifford was no longer on this Earth. Over time, the room became more and more comforting as the closest Walter could get to the love of his life was through these memories clinging to this space.

"Grampa!" an excited shriek burst through the air as a mess of thick tangled black hair and sequined clothing named Liv darted across the living room and leapt on Walter's lap. "Do you wanna know what I saw today?" she shrieked in delight, her eyes as big as her face.

"What did you saw today?" Walter replied playfully with a hearty laugh, Liv pulling his head close to share the secret of her discovery with Grampa.

"I saw a book about sharks in the library and I got it so we can read it," she let go of his head and adorned herself with those puppy-dog-like eyes that she wears so well when she wants something. Naturally, Walter would never decline the opportunity to read a book with his granddaughters. However, a well-known fact between his granddaughters is that their puppy-dog-eyes are his greatest weakness causing him to succumb to just about any request or demand, whether it be extra sprinkles on his famous ice cream shakes, or to stay up past their bedtime to watch more episodes of those old cartoons they love.

Melanie, his older granddaughter, and Alex, his son-in-law, followed Liv in through the front door. Melanie is of that age where angst drips from her, and coolness is everything. She recently decided to go by a much cooler 'Mel,' a fact Walter would often forget but would be quickly reminded by an eye roll and a sigh of exasperation. Today she carried a presentation foam-board but kept the display hidden from Walter's view.

"Hey, Grampa," she nodded like she usually does, only this time with a sly little smile like she was hiding something.

"Oh-ho, hello Mel," Walter said, heaving Liv back to the floor, and walking over to give the rest of the family a hug. "What do you have there?" Walter asked as he tapped gently on the foam board. Mel twisted around playfully to keep the board out of Walter's sight.

"You'll see!" she replied with her radiant smile, a sight that has been all the rarer since she entered her teenage years.

"She had a presentation today, and wants to share it with you," Alex chimed in, reaching over to hug Walter. "How're you doing today, Dad?"

"Another day in paradise," Walter replied with a smile.

Matt entered the room, making his way towards the door. The hands-on the gold anniversary clock on the shelf indicate that he stayed longer than usual. He must've had an in-depth conversation with Taylor. He exchanged pleasant greetings with Alex and hugs with Mel and Liv. Over the years he's become more like family than a care-taker, he even makes guest appearances on select holidays when he can get the chance.

"I'm taking off, Walter. I'll see you tomorrow," he said, hugging Walter. " Have fun on your big date tonight."

"Thank you, Matt," Walter smiled, as Matt opened the front door. "And Matt?"

"Yes," he asked, pausing in the doorframe.

"Message the girl," Walter said with his notorious cheeky smile.

Matt nodded with a grin. "Okay." He shut the door behind him.

The family gathered at the kitchen table which had been cleared by Taylor, as the smell of the rich flavors from Orlando's filled the home. Taylor was exactly like Clifford in the way that she knew exactly what everyone wanted and somehow knew exactly how to find the time to pick up an incredible meal while running in million-and-a-half directions. Discussion filled the room – reports on how the day went, school activities, accomplishments on daily assignments and grades, promotions at work, and exciting prospects paired perfectly with the meal. It never crossed his mind in his younger years, but as he's grown into his age, Walter has realized that moments like these are fleeting. All too soon, Mel will be in college, off on the opposite side of the country. Liv will join her sister in college shortly after that. Taylor and Alex will face a series of career changes, highs and lows, and rearranging schedules. All the while, dinners like this will become all the rarer, and unannounced visits will become fewer and farther between. The thought of that used to weigh heavy on his heart. Every time he would gather with his family, he would frantically try to create snapshots in his mind of what everyone looked like, what they said, what they were wearing. It got to the point that he was so frantic he forgot the most important piece of these gatherings: to enjoy the moment.

He has since learned that lesson, sitting at that table, enjoying every moment with his family, enjoying getting to know more about the incredible people who fill his life, and how lucky he is to have them.

After the dinner was over and the table cleared, the family resigned to the family room.

"Dad, you should let me take you furniture shopping this weekend. We can replace some of this bulky furniture and make this space feel bigger," Taylor urged, as she took a seat on the overstuffed sofa across from the armchair that Walter laid his bones in.

"Okay," Walter waved her off, not wanting to get into the discussion about furniture yet again. "We'll go," Walter offered, with every intention of telling her he didn't remember come Saturday when she comes to pick him up to go shopping.

Mel grabbed the board from the corner of the room and turned to face the family.

"So, I had to do this college admissions essay about something in our lives that inspires us, and my English teacher required us to do a visual representation of the essay . . ." Mel rolled her lips and avoided eye contact with everyone in the room. She's always been very uncomfortable with public presentations, even if it's just in front of family. With a hopeful sigh, she turned the board around and displayed it to the family.

Photos of Clifford and Walter spanning decades covered the bright pink board. Photos that Walter hasn't seen in years adorned the foam board, leaving him in awe of the project.

"I wrote my essay on the love that you and Grampa shared," she said softly. Tears began to swell in Walter's eyes.

In each of the snapshots that adorned the board, memories were jogged in Walter's head. The photo of the happy couple in front of their newly purchased home. The first photo of them and Taylor on her adoption day. Photos of various happy gatherings throughout decades jump-started a series of stories and anecdotes that left the family laughing and reminiscing. The granddaughters held tightly to each of the memories shared by Walter, and with each word, he realized the man that accompanied him on this crazy journey through life would continue to live on. He lives on in the laughs that fill this space. He'll live on when Mel and Liv begin families of their own, and the stories that Clifford and Walter penned through their lives will be passed down and shared in times of happiness, in times of sorrow. These stories will be used as a map as the family continues to navigate through uncharted territory, and they'll be paralleled with stories that they continue to create on their own. At this moment Walter realized that the photos that adorned his walls weren't just a series of moments frozen in time, but rather long brush strokes on the canvas of the story of their family, to be remembered, to be built upon, to be shared. At that moment, Walter realized to some extent what this life was all about.

As quickly as they came, the family left in order to get the girls to their various extra-curricular activities. The excitement of the day had dwindled, and Walter found himself in the same space he found himself every night . . . alone.

He tended to the same nightly rituals that had become routine as he readied his body for sleep. Walter changed out of his daily clothes, and into his pajamas. He washed his face, brushed his teeth, and made sure he was ready for bed before taking his nightly collection of pills and lozenges. An overwhelming sense that he had forgotten something had overcome him. He turned to his closet and laid out a suit – a suit that hadn't been worn in years. He picked a blue pocket square to match the undershirt. He picked out his lucky raven lapel pin that Clifford had given him years ago. He laid out the outfit in the chair in the corner of the room, all the while not being able to shake this feeling that he had forgotten something.

He finally came to rest on the edge of the bed, taking a deep sigh. He took in the details of his room, from the antique dresser, and the photos that adorned the top. He took in the nightstands and the decorations that had remained unchanged since Clifford and he had picked them out. He took in the rug that his feet laid on, eager to join the rest of his body in bed. Succumbing to their request, he maneuvered his legs one at a time into the sheets. He lowered himself slowly into the bed, the pressure of the day holding tightly to his lower back as he went, and gently lowered himself to his pillow. He reached his right arm up and turned off the night light next to his bed. He laid in the darkness for a moment before reaching his left arm out to feel the spot where Clifford used to lay – his final nighttime ritual. Secretly he had always wished that Clifford's hand would grab his back, but every night he went to sleep disappointed.

Walter fell asleep the same way he has for the last 83 years, slowly and then all at once. He tucked himself into the sailboat patterned sheets, gently pulling the sheets over him and giving the boats safe harbor for the night. Slowly he traced the fractured fractals and figments of faces he had found in the patterns of the plastered ceiling above him. The weight of the darkness laid heavy on his eyelids, ushering him to sleep. The adventures of the day had come to a close, and his body prepared him for the adventures of the next day, the daily activities scheduled out in advance. Eventually, the feeling of something forgotten resided washed away on the waves slowly pulling Walter away from the harbor of consciousness into the dark, gentle ocean of sleep.

And just as quickly he fell asleep, he was up. The world was still dark, with the exception of the clock on his nightstand, which gently illuminated the space with electric-green numbers: 1:36 AM. The grogginess of the early morning made it impossible for him to tell whether or not he was awake or dreaming. Despite his uncertainty, Walter remembered he had a date to get ready for, and couldn't keep himself anchored to the bed any longer. He pulled himself off the mattress with dreamlike ease, more rested than he had felt in ages, His excitement seemed to mask the pain he typically felt in his knees, his hips, and his back as he made his way to the bathroom.

Walter did his hair, pulling a wet comb through his hair.

Walter sprayed himself with the desert rose cologne he had purchased earlier, letting the mist hang gently in the air as he moved to the bedroom.

Walter put on the suit that laid on the chair with the same sense of excitement that enveloped him the last time he wore the suit. The buttons seemed to fall into place perfectly, without an ache of his hand. The vest slipped on perfectly, and the coat over the top. He noticed the rose from his coat he wore earlier laying on his dresser. He slipped it into his boutonniere and put his raven pin on the other lapel.

Walter stood in front of the mirror and took in the image of the man who stood in front of him. Although the years have clung to him as he navigated through this journey, he never felt so young, and much to his surprise he hadn't looked so young. He admired the black tailored suit and the raven on his lapel. He hadn't felt this confident in years. At this moment, Walter had never been so ready.

"After all these years, you still take my breath away," a voice from the bedroom door cut through the morning silence.

"I almost thought you weren't going to show," Walter replied, turning to face the man who stood in the doorway.

There he stood. Just as beautiful as the day they had met. His brilliant blue-green eyes made time come to a stop, the same way they did when he was 16. He stood there, dressed in an identical suit to Walter, which was no surprise – they would often find themselves in the same outfits by accident. For years, Walter had planned what he would say when he got the chance to see him again. He had it perfectly scripted, but at this moment Walter found himself speechless in the deafening magnetism that pulled the two together. It's the same magnetism that pulled the two through decades of this world together, braving the good, the bad, and everything in between that the universe threw at them. It had been a while since Walter felt that feeling, but for the first time in 10 years, he didn't feel alone.

"After all these years, you still take my breath away," Walter finally found the strength to say.

The man extended his hand, beckoning Walter to him, and Walter obliged, practically floating across the floor, taking his hand in his, happiness so profound hadn't been felt by either of the men in nearly a decade.

"You ready?" the man asked with the same radiant smile that continues to melt Walter's heart, shining brighter now than it ever did in his memories.

"Clifford, I've never been more ready," Walter replied.

The two walked down the hallway, past all the faces in the frames of the memories that they had built together, only now they feel so much happier than they did yesterday morning. The creaky old floorboards of the home they built together laid in silence underneath them as they made their way through the home one last time. The memories that hung in the air like dust burst like fireworks around the two, celebrating the reunion of the greatest love story ever told. The two men stood in the home one last time, standing on the edge of eternity the same way they faced their lives together: fearless.

"You know, you forgot to turn off the coffee pot," Clifford informed Walter with a boyish grin that never seemed to age.

"I knew I forgot something."

Who Will Be My Love?

K. A. Baker

Phoenix, Arizona - United States

Usually, we learn about some event, much after it has already occurred. And it could be many days or many months and sometimes, years. This is due to the simple fact, we can't be in all places at all times. Then we are left to wonder, in amazement. What were the universal forces in effect that allowed this wonderful event to materialize so magically, before us?

Sheri was a college graduate with loads of dating experience. She had dating experience with many diverse kinds of guys. Some even were perhaps considered men. Some were just considered, men about town. She was a very smart cookie however and always knew how to handle any given situation. No matter how difficult or strange.

One of these candidates had a great deal to offer any woman. Just ask him, he would tell you. He was employed as a professor at the college. Great salary. Housing would never be an issue. Nor a healthy dose of ego. Travel would always be able to be planned out ahead, maybe even twice per year. How many chicks would jump at that? We'll find out. She found out a couple things shortly into their dating span. Prior to this, she never even knew about his drinking behaviors. But she was curious. He would typically have a drink, or two, when they would dine out. Always vodka and tonic or gin and tonic. Never brown or amber colored stuff . . . or never just a beer or a glass of wine.

On one of their dates, "Jerry" had to make an unscheduled stop at his place. He had told her he forgot about something that must be dealt with, right away. So, when they arrived, he asked her to come in and wait for him in the living room, so she would not have to wait in the car for the 10 minutes or so this would probably take.

Comfortable, (sort of) in the living room she was told, "Please hang out here, this should not take very long." That is when she decided to start her investigative work. Opening cupboards and finding bottles in places where one would usually not store such items. Snooping has been around for a long, long time. Strange that not one bottle was out somewhere in plain sight, where most grownups would put them. So back quickly to the sofa.

Then all at once the bedroom door opens and Jerry emerges forth. Completely nude. Walks past her and right on into the kitchen as if she were not even there. Only to return a moment later, then pause and face her, quite openly and ask, "Oh, by the way, did I tell you that I am an active nudist and was hoping you would be fine with that. We are all adults here, right?" She was already jumping to her feet by this time and as she bolted to the front door, screamed back, "NO!" you've not brought that up yet! And NO, THAT is not alright with me! AND PLEASE, FOR GOD'S

SAKE, LOSE MY PHONE NUMBER!" as she slammed the door behind her.

She called her friend from a pay phone to get a ride back home.

Another guy she had dated for an abbreviated time invited her for a picnic out on the lake. He had a motorboat. She was always up for a picnic. Sheri loved planning little side trips and events that would be off into the future. This man was a pretty good person overall. Self-reliant and hardworking, talented in many ways. A very creative type. A musician. The only problem, he was pretty much out for himself. He preferred being single, a bit of a loner. Not a strong communicator either. Because of that, he did not find out until they were out in the middle of the lake that she was not as crazy about him as he was about her. Let's be honest here. He was trying to impress and score on this gal. She was thinking they would be boating to some point that had a nice quiet beach where they would be getting out of the boat and setting up the picnic. You know, blankets, wine, talk and such. He was thinking they would find a nice, secluded place way out on the lake or perhaps a nice quiet little cove with no one else around. Then crack open some wine and let the romance commence. Well Sheri was very flattered about his attempt. She delicately and politely helped him to understand that she was not really into him that way. As in romantically interested. Well, the wolfman completely understood and knew this was not going to go his way. He being a good sport about their newfound relationship, and they ended up having a nice time for the rest of the day, with no sexual tension and a few laughs thrown in on the side. They even remained good friends over the next several years. They would occasionally meet at different concerts and catch up on each other's lives.

So as Sheri's love life trudges on, she is now much less concerned about when she is going to meet her next love interest and begins to focus more on her own personal growth. Not to follow a fad, but to get herself into a better, happier mindset within herself. Besides, she was scheduled for a trip to the west coast for work. The best part of the trip was looking forward to a visit to the beach. One of her favorite things to do. She has loved the ocean's edge for a long time. She truly loved the magical powers this part of the Earth had over her senses and her psyche.

On her final day, work ended at noon. YIPPEE! She had several hours for one more trip to the beach. She loved watching the seagulls, the crashing waves, the children as they fascinated over this amazing part of their world. It was late afternoon, and she was feeling somewhat melancholy. She had been alone for most of this trip. Watching all the people on the beach reminded her again of not being with that special someone. As she stared off toward the glistening horizon, she had an idea. She went in search of a stick. Something to make a drawing with. She finds just the right branch from some bushes. Goes back over to the area she was enjoying so peacefully. Most of the other people have gone by now. She went to just the right place in the sand where it had enough moisture to make her drawing, and waves did not quite reach as yet. She knew the waves would be coming in further as the tide would begin to rise.

She begins making this heart shape in the sand with her artist stick. It needed to be big enough to write in her inscription that she saw in her mind's eye minutes earlier. She carefully writes the words that would be carried out to sea as the waves would later come and do that for her. Then she finds a nice comfortable place to relax and wait. Enjoying her final few hours, as she stared off into the waves and the distant horizon. After several daydreams and many lovely thoughts as she watched the shore's edge, she noticed the first wave that came in and kissed the top edge of her artwork. Knowing now that the entire piece of art would be carried out into the ocean in a matter of minutes. She would stay and wait for this little project to be complete. One fourth of the heart is now gone. She realized the waves would start washing it away from the edge closest to the waves. Knowing this, when she made the drawing, she drew it up-side down. The top words would be taken in the order they were – written. Sheri knew what she was doing when it came to asking the universe for help. Word by word, her question would be taken out into the ocean.

WHO

WILL BE

MY

LOVE?

And the universe can decide when I shall have my answer.

She was turning this part of her life over to a much higher pow-er. She had experienced the power of the universe before in her life, during times of need. . . . it was now time to go back to the hotel.

What a beautiful day she has had. Now she must go back to the hotel, to gather her things and her suitcase and get to the airport for the flight back home. Mom and Dad would be there to meet her at the baggage claim then drive her back home to her cozy little one-bedroom apartment.

Mom and Dad were as reliable as dirt. They were always ready, willing and able to be there when Sheri needed their help. They were your typical middle-class folks. Strong of character and true to their word with everybody that came into their circle. To stay or those just passing through. As they gave each other loving hugs and kisses on the cheeks, Sheri saw her bag. "There it is Dad! Please help me." Before her Dad could even make his move, a handsome business class man jumped into action. He grabs the suitcase with ease and as he hands it to her, "Anything for you my dear" he says. Sheri just chuckles and gives him a look like. "Nice try Jack, I'm not giving you my number." Dad comes in and accepts the bag from the kind gentleman and they scamper off toward the car. As they are walking along chatting as folks often will, from behind a column out strolls ME! "Hi SHERI!" "How was your trip"? "Did everything go well"? Sheri was absolutely beside herself with surprise and so happy to see me. "HI DARLING!" she belts out. "I'm so glad to see you, what a very pleasant surprise that (you) would be here." She looks at her parents and ask, "Did you know he was here?" Her Mom and Dad snicker and Mom says, "Yes, He sort of came along for the ride. He wanted to be here. We just couldn't say no." Well, Sheri thought it was great. She was so happy, and her spirit was soaring so she could not stop smiling the entire ride back home. In the car she would not let go of my hand. And the smile on her face, every time she looked at me. Well, it was pure medicine to me.

She finally told me the beach drawing story 3 or 4 months later on one of our many dates. She told me, "That's why I was so happy to see you that night my darling." (At the airport) "Now I was a part of her story, a part of her life," I thought with a solid grin on my face. These are the moments that will stick with us, in our minds and our hearts for the rest of our life as the days just keep on rolling, along. If we are lucky. So, the universe chose me. I would be her love. We were married in just under 3 years from that day.

So cast your fate to the wind the next time you have a conundrum. Or go to the beach and let the waves carry your message out to the universe via the ocean's waves. Sometimes it really does work.

Love Of My Life

Roy Kindelberger

Edmonds, Washington - United States

snowfall closes

the mountain pass in the winter

north cascades

in hibernation

our love continues

Summer's end. The soft breeze drifts through the mountain air. Leaves begin to fall. Twin beauties loom in the blue skies. Mount Baker and Shuksan. Below, the rolling waters of the deceptive Skagit River. Lakes nestled in valleys. Wooded trails meander through the tree filled woods. Destination…doesn't matter. We take a selfie to say we were here.

love of my life
even when we were
oceans apart
i hold her in my arms
forever…and ever

One Night

Kieran McLoughlin

Redmond, Washington - United States

It was three AM,
I see the somber, cold sky with clouds lifelessly passing by
two stars and countless planes in the sky hovering above
a smoke has tainted the air in this small neighborhood
lingering.
A dark street containing a light leading me home
my heart was cold,
and I was alone.

but the stroke of that old clock made me feel minuscule,
in this small neighborhood,
I sit in a chair with a sweater that makes me look small
with shorts that show my bare thighs and a white tee
stained by that night of fun parting and torn memories...'

I saw you Leave
your flannel told me your story
but disappeared
I chased,
a stranger
you,
On a bench alone
I sat next to you
your hair falling off your face, revealing your structured façade
and so, did I
that night
filled with discomfort dialogue, and fearful whispers
your Voice glided into my Ears
into my bones
into me.

small talk formed
awkward jokes
long walks to your house,
laughing our eyes away,
one night,
it was cold out
my senses were shattered
but you were there in the rain

standing tall
just in time
to put me back together.

clothes were taken
your flannel was 'lost.'
and you stole mine,
we ran and collapsed on that hill
and laughed our sorrows away,
then they were gone
and we didn't even notice.

Dancing in the living room,
late-night breakfasts,
long walks home
we cry, and we embrace
we doubt and trust
we battle and die for each other
but we cling to each other
as we drop our weapons and let it trickle and fall.

"I love you,"
you whispered to me one night
the flush on your face after those words left your rosy lips

your soft and delicate voice echoed from those short moons

made me warm

a long pause sat between us

while looking away down at our feet, I whispered back

"I love you, too"

both our cheeks bleed into that bench as we stare at that emerald
beacon

a realization kicked in

we were together.

those late-night instants

have been everything to us

from our great battles to our silent nights

it makes us who we are and, I wouldn't want to change anything

"I love you."

we held hands

stole each other's breath

and ran to our classic car with rice in our hair

and sped off, leaving everything behind,

the dark sky with tiny hearts sprinkled across the sky,

the smell of flowers,

us was all that remained.

It is now that
I have endured another melancholy night
of trying to form these words
with an oversized sweater that swallowed my body,
a stained white shirt,
and shorts that exposed my legs and thighs
in this chair, with this device
in this dark room
writing about
"love"
that began at the darkest corner of the night
with lavender haze
filling my brain
and growing into a flower
that will be plucked from my head for a 'special day.'

Acknowledgements

Annie Duyen Tran

C.W. Toledo

Kieran McLoughlin

Danielle Chan

Participants In Contest

Annie Duyen Tran

Meghan Giannotta

Danielle Chan

Micah Brocker

Rose McCoy

Hayley Hylton

C.W. Toledo

Kenneth A. Baker

Roy Kindelberger

Kieran McLoughlin

Winners

Hayley Hylton

C.W. Toledo

Kenneth A. Baker

Dear Reader,

We are ecstatic to note that you chose to read one of our publications. The time you invested into reading this book is much appreciated. We value your allegiance. As a give back present, we will be happy to share **'YOUR PICTURE HOLDING THIS BOOK'** on our *Official Social Media Handles* such as Facebook, Instagram and Twitter.

All you have to do is – send it to us.

1. Write Your Name

2. Review, if any

3. Subject Line of Email – Pic Holding Book (Book Name)

4. Image Attached – jpeg / gif/ png file.

Email it to – visions.visionary@gmail.com

Gift A Copy Of This Book To A Friend

Now, you can send a copy to a friend you want to surprise.
Place an order of the book with us on our website.

After placing an order, email us.

Email – visions.visionary@gmail.com

Subject Line of Email – Gift A Copy To A Friend

In your email, please specify –

- Name and address of your friend. Make sure the address has the pin code, contact number and email id.
- If it is on an occasion, like a birthday, please specify, we will insert a birthday wish for them.
- A note, if any, that you'd like us to insert.
- Share with us, why do you consider the book a perfect present for the person receiving the book, if possible.
- Your Name, as you'd like us to mention for your friend to know it is from you.
- Name of the book you placed an order for – so that we are sure we are sending the book you intend to send to the person this gift is meant for.

Send Us A Book Review

Now, you can send us your written or video – *book review.*

If it is a written review, we will use your review in the book when it goes for a reprint, with your name included. So, please do remember to specify your name.

If it is a video, we will showcase your video on our Youtube Channel. Do subscribe to our Youtube Channel 'Poets Choice' for more. You can reach us your video review via email.

Email – visions.visionary@gmail.com

Subject – Video/Written Book Review _____(Name of Book)

Please try to include, in your email –

1. The date you purchased the book.
2. The name of the author you found most adorable, in case of an anthology.
3. What was your take away.
4. Why did you like/dislike our book.
5. What makes you come back to us.
6. Is there anything you find *different*, something that is specific or unique in our books, something that stands out.